Lights drew h‹ [barcode] the mill, where a m. ... her. Breath caught in her lungs as she froze.

But only for a brief moment until she realized it wasn't a man, at least not a living one. Her breath escaped on a whoosh of relief. Intuition whispered the man was the spirit who'd watched her last night.

The one from her dream.

Shadows clung to his body, ghostly fingers releasing as he stepped into the dim slash of moonlight. Lights flickered from behind him, like the dying gasps of sputtering candles. Dressed in a white shirt with an old-fashioned high collar, sleeves rolled halfway up his forearms, and dark trousers, he reminded her of a working man in a World War I photograph. As if he had removed his coat and tie and rolled up his sleeves to get to work.

Except the men in those photos didn't sport the wide-eyed, happy look of this man. Ghost. Whatever. Yeah, he wasn't the only one surprised. She'd sworn never to see a ghost again, yet there stood a ghost, captured by her gaze. The man was hot, in an old-fashioned way. At least he didn't sport a handle-bar moustache.

He gestured to her, his hand beckoning in a "come here" motion.

She squeezed the bridge of her nose. Was she actually thinking of heading his way? Judging by the way her feet pointed toward the door, she'd already decided. Dammit. She might not want to see a ghost or speak to a spirit, but past experience told her if she ignored them, they ramped up the annoying factor.

How bad could it be to talk to an attractive spirit?

The Shadowheart Curse

by

Karilyn Bentley

This is a work of fiction. Names, characters, places, and incidents are either the product of the author's imagination or are used fictitiously, and any resemblance to actual persons living or dead, business establishments, events, or locales, is entirely coincidental.

The Shadowheart Curse

COPYRIGHT © 2019 by Karilyn Bentley

The Wild Rose Press, Inc.
PO Box 708
Adams Basin, NY 14410-0708
Visit us at www.thewildrosepress.com

Publishing History
First Black Rose Edition, 2019
Print ISBN 978-1-5092-2773-0
Digital ISBN 978-1-5092-2774-7

Published in the United States of America

Dedication

To my husband:
Thank you for your love and support!
To Rhonda:
Thank you for giving me this opportunity.
It's appreciated more than you can know.

Chapter One

You have arrived, the GPS app announced.

For the first time since she turned the app on at the airport in Rome, the overly perky voice failed to elicit a teeth-grinding response. Amazing. Not her lack of response, but the place nestled before her in a copse of trees.

Adrianna Sinclair gawked at the ruined mill. Was this awesome building really on her family's ancestral property? She checked the address on the GPS against the address in her email. Yep. The same.

Midafternoon sun beamed through the copse of trees and danced along light brown stones. Green vines with lush leaves crept around the corners of the edifice while dappled light played peek-a-boo with the stones hidden behind the greenery. Two towers sat in the middle of the ruin with water-stained crenellations reaching toward the sky like arms lifted heavenward for help. One side of the mill had been remodeled with a thick slab of steel for the roof. The other half remained in ruins.

Wow. Just. Wow.

She opened the rental car door and slowly stepped out, resting one arm on the door, her gaze snagged on the ancient structure. Humidity wrapped around her like a heavy blanket in the heat of the afternoon sun. The scent of late summer grass and crushed vegetation filled her nose. Tension eased from her muscles as a warm breeze wrapped around her like a soft blanket.

Umbria, Italy, in the summer never failed to relax her. Escaping here was a great idea.

A squeal of joy caused her to turn to the side, where an older couple jumped out of a car. A car she should have noticed driving up, but holy smokes, the mill captured her attention like a poltergeist on a rampage.

She focused on the older couple heading her way. A smile crept across her face. The caretakers, Luigi and Maria Toscano, had been married for more years than she could ever dream of and were more like family than hired help. Luigi met her gaze, his mouth mirroring her smile. The gray-haired, plump Maria darted around their car, past her husband, and enveloped her in a hug.

"Oomph." The hug came close to smothering her, but at least she had no doubt she was welcomed.

Which was a nice change from what she'd left behind.

"Maria!" She wrapped her arms around the short, matronly woman and squeezed. *Home. Maria feels like home.*

"Let me look at you." Maria stepped back, holding her at arm's length. Her brown eyes looked her up and down. She *tsked*. "Too skinny. And you look tired. We'll fix both those problems. Some good food. A little rest. But first you must see the mill."

Luigi limped across the short distance between the cars. When had he started limping? Once he reached them, he enveloped her in a large hug. Another confirmation she'd made the correct decision to leave New York City for Italy.

"Look at you, look at you." Luigi patted her on the back before releasing her. He stepped back and like his wife, let his gaze rake her from head to toe and back again. "You've grown up."

A smile played across her lips. Her Italian so rusty from several years of little to no practice, but it would come back. The out-of-use words wrapped around her tongue as she spoke. "That's what happens when fifteen years go by."

"Fifteen years?" Maria shook her head. "It's been that long?"

Hard to believe she'd spent so long without visiting her family's land. Her land now. Sort of. She shared the title with cousins she only corresponded with on rare occasions and barely remembered from her youth.

Coming to Italy had multiple benefits, including escaping New York City, catching up with relatives, and learning about property maintenance. Not that she was expected to grab a hoe and hack at a grapevine, or whatever one did with a hoe. No, as the property managers, that was the Toscanos' expertise.

Although she suspected they no longer wielded hoes.

"I'm sorry. I shouldn't have stayed away so long, but life got busy." She hid a yawn behind her hand. The nine-hour flight from New York to Rome, then driving for over an hour was catching up to her. Not to mention the time change. She might be hungry and looking forward to anything Maria cooked, but she'd really prefer to crash for the rest of the day.

"You haven't been back since you went off to university." Maria glared while Luigi nodded.

Fifteen years. Time flew. Hadn't she just been

seventeen yesterday, eager to start college and be an adult? Adulting wasn't as fun as her seventeen-year-old self had imagined.

Hoping her smile erased Maria's shaming glare, Adrianna patted the older woman's arm. "I know. I'm sorry. College was busy. And then Grandfather died. And work got crazy." And the Very Bad Thing happened. Hopefully Maria and Luigi hadn't read any of the papers from New York City. Or the internet, tabloids, or gossip rags.

Their English might not be the best, but anyone could hit the translate button on internet news articles and discover the main reason New York City was no longer her city of choice. Being questioned in a murder investigation while having one's face and name splashed across all media outlets tended to do that to a person. She'd gone from being a well-known medium to a second-rate psychic overnight.

All her fault.

She shook her head. Nope. Not getting into it. Italy was her escape. Her perfect home. A permanent vacation to another life.

"Tell me about the mill." She gestured to the moss-covered stone ruins.

A spark lit their eyes as they looked toward the mill, excitement and pride written across the lines of their faces. Maria spoke. "You know we sold the manor house, yes?"

She nodded. She hated to hear that news, but times changed, and while the vineyards and farming properties were profitable, they were not profitable enough to keep up repairs on the sixteenth-century house. She missed the place, but she understood why it needed to be sold. Apparently, the new owners had turned it into an online rental home.

"For centuries, people from all around brought their grain here"—Maria gestured to the ruined building—"for the waterwheel to grind. We knew the stories, how industrialization at the turn of the last century had put most of the mills out of business, and they were left abandoned. But we could never find the mill. It couldn't have been part of the manor house because there wasn't a stream close enough to it. And yet there are stories."

She blinked. Stories? About mills? She couldn't remember hearing any interesting tales about mills, but then again, she'd flown nine hours to Rome, grabbed a rental car, and made it here without falling asleep at the wheel. That accomplishment depleted her last reserve of brain power. "Stories?"

"Many stories. Your grandfather didn't tell you about them?"

Had he? It wasn't like she remembered every single conversation she'd ever had with him. "If he did, I don't remember. But it's beautiful." Her eyes narrowed. "Wait a minute. How could you or my family not know where the mill stood? I know it's a huge property, but still. Wouldn't someone have seen it?"

"You'd think." Excitement turned Maria's speech into a rush of words. "But the land reclaimed it. Trees were growing through everything. We left some of the vines, as you can see." She gestured to the vines spilling from the partially collapsed roof. "The whole thing was overgrown. It took forever to clean it up and make it presentable."

"Okay." The place retained enough of a "buried in a forest" look for her believe Maria's explanation, despite how odd it seemed not to know such a large building existed on the estate. "How did you find it?"

A gleam shone from Luigi's eyes. "We went exploring."

"You did the exploring yourselves?" Adrianna looked from one to the other. Fifteen years ago, she wouldn't have asked the question.

Maria waved a hand. "No, no. Several years ago, after your sweet grandfather passed and we had sold the manor house, we were approached by an enterprising young man with one of those drones. He wanted permission to fly it over our land—"

"He was one of those archeologists. Looking for abandoned mills."

When Luigi took a breath, Maria finished the story. "And he found one. On our property. The mill of the stories."

"And we've turned it into a bed and breakfast." Luigi looked as if he'd found a rent-stabilized apartment in the Bronx.

"You have?" Had they told her that when they offered to let her stay here?

Maria glared at Luigi. "Not yet. We'd like you to try it out first. You said you didn't know how long you wanted to stay. We thought you might rather stay here for free than at a hotel."

They were right. This place was cool, and she'd have some much-needed time to herself. Being alone would give her time to think and strategize her future. Judging by the way nausea roiled her gut each time she thought of returning to New York and continuing her work as a medium, she needed a new life plan.

"That would be great. Is it an apartment or just a room?"

"An apartment. Kitchenette and bathroom." Maria gestured to their left. "The pool is over there."

She glanced toward the pool, but before she got a good look, Maria pointed to the trunk of the car. "Luigi, grab her bag."

Before the older man could move, she fast-stepped to her trunk and popped it open. She grabbed her suitcase, heaved the heavy luggage out of the trunk, and jumped back as it fell on the grass with a soft thud, narrowly missing her foot.

"Luigi, hurry up." Maria clapped her hands twice. "A tiny thing like her can't be expected to lift a suitcase."

She managed to stop an eye roll. Tiny thing? Yeah, right. She was thin but stayed in shape by lifting weights, swimming, and weekly Tae Kwon Do classes. Or at least she had until her poor advice made her want to flee the Big Apple. Running away from problems instead of meeting them head on was a new one for her, but everyone needed to try something different once in a while.

She shook her head. Not thinking about it. Her one-way ticket to Italy came with a deal to not think about what had happened in New York.

At least for the moment.

Before Luigi could grab her luggage, she pulled up the handle, tilted the suitcase onto its wheels, and yanked it across the grass toward the ruins. No way was she letting an elderly man carry the heavy thing. And when had Luigi gotten so old? The last time she saw him, he'd looked like he could pick up a sumo wrestler and pitch him across the gym. Now? Now she doubted he could pick up the wrestler's head gear.

Luigi fell into step beside her, shrugging at Maria's glare.

"This place is amazing."

Created from brown and white stones, the mill boasted two towers in the middle with an arched bridge between them. A sloped tunnel entrance under the bridge paid homage to a dried-out stream bed once diverted to power the mill. The left wing had been renovated to contain the apartment; the right remained in ruins. Tunnels ran underneath both wings, their darkened entrances resembling the black eyes of a demon.

Trees encroached upon the back of the building. At one time, vines overran the entire structure, but most of those had been removed during the cleanup, leaving behind artfully arranged greenery in the corners, falling like a trellis from the roof. A thick metal slab served as a roof and covered the top of the ruin above the apartment.

An amazing feat considering the structure was originally built in the sixteenth century without the advancements of modern construction equipment.

They walked toward the mill, veering to the left side. A wooden door with a window to the right of it greeted them. Her sneakers crunched on the gravel patio as she drew in a breath heavy with the rich scent of fresh flowers. A bench with metal trim and wood slats sat under a window surrounded by flowerpots containing bright blooms of red, yellow, and white. Across from the bench stood a black, metal, trident lamppost.

Luigi pulled a key out of his pocket, unlocked the door and shoved it open. He handed her the key, then he and Maria stepped back, allowing her to pull her suitcase into the room.

"Wow! This is great!" She looked around the room. A queen-sized bed with ornately designed walnut head and footboards was covered in a white bedspread. Matching marble-topped nightstands sat on either side of the bed. Cherubim holding lampshades stood on the nightstands. A large rug covered the brown-tiled floor under the bed.

She set her suitcase on the mattress and turned in a half circle. A table surrounded by four chairs sat to her right. Behind the table, sunk deep into the wall, was a window which overlooked the not-yet-renovated wing. A fireplace bereft of logs sat on the wall next to the table, with a glass frame containing her family's crest hanging above the mantel. Two comfy-looking chairs faced the hearth as if waiting for the warmth of crackling wood. A dresser sat on the wall perpendicular to the fireplace.

She walked to the door left of the bed and pushed it open, poking her head inside. A bathroom. Always good to know where those were located. Closing the door, she glanced at the small kitchenette between the bathroom and the front door and back to Maria.

A smile spread across her face.

Maria clasped her hands together. "I'm glad you like it."

"Like it? I love it! You really don't mind me staying here?"

"No, no. It's not totally fixed up." She glanced at

Luigi, an unreadable expression passing between them.

What did that glance mean? Maybe they had construction issues. As long as she had running water and an indoor toilet, she was good.

"You unpack while we get dinner out of the car." Maria gestured to the dresser. "I cooked lasagna for us. We can eat and talk about what's been going on with you."

Once they left, she busied herself unpacking clothes, placing the items in the dresser under the front window. She hung her dresses on the small rack in the bathroom. The lip balm, chargers, and e-reader she placed in the drawer of the nightstand next to a flashlight. *Click-click.* She pushed the button on the flashlight, turning it on and off. She had just placed her suitcase in the corner of the room when the Toscanos returned.

As soon as they put the food on the table, a cold breeze swept through the room, ruffling her hair. Maria and Luigi's eyes widened as they glanced at each other. Small hairs prickled her nape like fingernails scratching across her skin. The cold draft only meant one thing, and it wasn't a blast from the air conditioner. She doubted this place even had an AC.

No, the cold air meant a pissed-off spirit raced around her room. If she tried, she could see the thing, but she'd decided to no longer interact with ghosts shortly after being released from the police interrogation room. Which meant she was no longer working as a medium.

Bam! They all jumped as one of the nightstand lamps fell onto the floor.

Yep, a seriously pissed-off spirit.

Another gust of cold air swirled through the room. She felt the clash, the fight, even though she refused to allow herself to look at the swarming specters.

Why couldn't they leave her alone? *Because spirits are attracted to mediums.* She knew the reason, yet a break every once in a while would be nice. Especially when she'd sworn never to converse with one again.

She took a deep breath, marched to the nightstand, and placed the lamp upright where it belonged. At least the golden cherub remained in one piece. Cold stung her hand, residue from the entity tingling her palm. Never a good sign. Closing her eyes, she focused on centering her thoughts, on stopping the chill from traveling up her arm. Before she opened her eyes, warmth returned to the room, the cold air vanishing like it appeared, sudden and without warning.

Maria held her fingers over her gaping mouth while Luigi pressed a hand against his chest. Their pale cheeks slowly regained color. Maria recovered first, crossing herself as if that would help protect her from an angry specter hellbent on destruction.

Did they know an evil spirit inhabited the place? Or were they as surprised as she was? "Something you want to tell me?"

Another meaningful glance between the couple. Luigi shrugged. "It's an old mill. We have ghosts."

She raised a brow. "Those weren't just ghosts." Ghosts did not leave behind a cold residue that caused tingles to creep across her flesh. She rubbed her hand on her jeans, trying to wipe away the sensation.

"No?"

"No. At least one of them was demonic."

Maria's eyes widened as she crossed herself again.

"You're saying a demon haunts this place?"

"Not a demon. Not exactly." Massaging her still-tingling hand, she shook her head. "If a spirit was an evil person in life, like a murderer, it crosses over into death. The spirit becomes demonic. Most spirits are neutral."

What would cause two spirits, one of them evil, to haunt an abandoned, ruined mill? Most spirits haunted their own homes. Or an item they had been attached to while alive. Mills weren't on the list of the top-ten places to haunt. So why were they here?

A shiver shook her spine. Maybe she could find a local psychic to take care of the problem. Whoever the spirits were, they no longer swarmed through the apartment. Thank the gods. No matter how tired she was, she would put a ward around the apartment. No evil entity was going to hurt her tonight.

She offered the wide-eyed couple a grin. "I'm starving. Let's eat."

Chapter Two

Luca Fausto stared at the new arrival to his home. If one could call the ruined mill a home. More like a cage for the last century. A pretty young woman with large brown eyes and dark hair falling in curls to the middle of her back stood by a car. She looked about his age. Or at least his age before he'd been cursed into this ghost-like body. A curse that left him unable to leave this godforsaken estate.

Well, the estate wasn't godforsaken. But God had surely forsaken him, abandoning him to this half life. Always seeing, unable to leave the perimeters of the property, unable to grow old. Unable to make himself seen by the living.

Damn curse.

He moved closer to the woman and the caretakers as they walked across the grass to the mill. As usual, they didn't notice him. A sigh escaped his lips. He should be used to the lack of attention by the living, but every time he came into contact with them, the same annoying tightening of his chest and ache in his stomach made him realize he still held out hope.

Accepting this hated existence was hard. A litany of if-onlys danced through his mind. The same recitation that played over and over for decades. Shoving the bothersome thoughts to the side, he shook his head. He could if-only himself until the universe

13

died, and he would still be stuck here.

Madonna save him.

He sighed once again. Like God, Mother Mary wanted nothing to do with him.

On the positive side—and he really should be thinking on the positive side of things instead of falling into a moving sea of depression—he had some company. If one could call floating around a property filled with people who didn't know he existed company.

How you saw things was all in the mind, according to a book he read many years ago. Of course, that author had never experienced life as a spirit, but still.

Positive thoughts, Luca, positive thoughts.

He followed the three into the mill, remembering the first time he'd left it as a ghost. On that day, he'd strode inside as a man but flown away as a haunted spirit. A little hard to keep a positive attitude with that memory front and foremost.

Positive thoughts, Luca, positive thoughts. For instance, he'd "lived" well over a hundred years. Had seen many things despite being stuck on these grounds. Lucky for him, he could enter any of the structures associated with the property at the time of his curse. Even though the manor house had been sold, he could still enter it because it once sat on the original property. The place wasn't as interesting now; a constant stream of strangers rented the house, leaving little reading material behind.

In the past, entering the manor house and strolling through its halls had kept him up on the times. And the times had changed. Drastically. He might be a cursed spirit, but he could still read newspapers and the extensive books scattered throughout the place. It had required some time to learn how to focus his energy so his fingers didn't go straight through the pages. Now he was adept at moving things around.

He followed the three to his former office, the exact location where the curse had occurred. He shook himself, trying to erase the memory, to no avail. So much for positive thoughts. Maria and Luigi had hired a team of construction workers to turn the office into a beautiful apartment. Another rental, if he'd heard them correctly. Further proof of the changing times.

The older couple left the apartment, leaving the pretty woman alone. He leaned against the wall, watching her unpack clothes that looked nothing like what women had worn in his time. No complaints from him about women's clothing choices in this century. He liked watching them move in the body-freeing clothes.

He particularly liked watching this woman move, watching as emotions flickered across her face. What was she thinking?

She carried several pieces of clothing over her arm to the bathroom. He drifted closer as she grabbed hangers from the small rack and hung up her dresses. Her very short dresses. What he wouldn't give to see her in those with her long, tanned legs. Better yet she could wrap those legs—

Stop it, Luca! Giving himself a mental smack to dislodge the wayward thought, he walked through the door she'd closed and resumed his position of leaning against the wall.

A small wrinkle turned her brow as she carried a load of clothes to the dresser. Was she wondering where to put all the items? Perhaps she wondered how so many clothes could fit in her one suitcase? A feat of magic if he ever saw one.

If only she could see him. If only she could touch him. If only.

God Almighty. There he went again with all the damn if-onlys.

The woman zipped the suitcase closed, set it on its wheels, and shoved it beside the dresser right as Maria and Luigi returned with a carrier full of food. The older couple busied themselves putting the food on the table, but he paid them no mind, his attention focused on the woman. Flickering rays of sunlight through the window caught on her ring, shooting sparks off the stone to dance around the walls. The red stone glowed with inhuman light.

He froze. He remembered that stone. Set in a ring worn by his former employer, the red stone with the Romani family crest was part of his last memory while alive. He could never forget the memory. Or the stone. What were the chances the pretty woman wore Dario's ring? His stomach turned into a pulsing ball as if a thousand wings fluttered against fragile walls.

After all these years, was his curse at an end?

"What are you doing?"

He jumped at his brother's voice. He wasn't the only one cursed to a half life of existence.

"Marco."

"I asked what you were doing." Marco glared at him.

He glared back. A palm's width shorter than him with dark hair and eyes the color of a cloudy night sky, his brother nonetheless managed to loom over him. At one time he'd idolized his older brother. When they'd lived. When they'd worked together at the mill. Until the aftermath of the curse changed their relationship.

And not for the better.

Luca gestured to the attractive woman. "There's a visitor."

His brother turned to the woman. "So?"

He shrugged, refusing to mention the ring the woman wore. That was a secret he'd prefer to keep to himself. Since she had shifted out of the light and red sparks no longer flickered along the walls, unless he mentioned it, Marco should not be drawn to the ring.

"Are you going to welcome her, brother? Or stand staring?"

He narrowed his eyes at Marco's tone and the implication behind his words. "How would I welcome her? In case you forgot, we cannot speak to the living."

"Speak to them?" His brother shook his head, a sneer turning his upper lip. "Why would we do that?"

With the speed of a strong wind, Marco flew across the room and knocked the lamp off the nightstand. The crash of the lamp elicited gasps and shocked glares. Which was, undoubtedly, the response Marco wanted. Fear from the living. As if he fed off the reaction. Fingers balled into tight fists, he stepped toward his brother.

Marco darted around him toward the narrow-eyed woman. Why wasn't she running out the door at the threat? Or standing frozen in place like the Toscanos, pale and trembling? Couldn't she sense the anger flowing from his brother?

But he had no time to puzzle her reaction. Nostrils flaring, Marco raised his hand as if to strike her, an inhuman growl tearing from his lips. Without hesitation, he dashed to his brother, his arm cocked, and slammed his fist into Marco's jaw, knocking his brother back a step. Marco roared, head-butting him through the wall and onto the graveled patio. If he were human, the pointed rocks would have hurt like hell, but as a ghost he only felt a mild discomfort. It hurt worse for Marco to land a punch.

Before he could rise, Marco leapt through the stone wall and landed on top of him. He squirmed out of his grasp, shoving him off the patio to drop the few feet onto the grass. Marco rolled as soon as he hit the ground, and Luca jumped on top of him, pummeling his fists into his brother's face. The fight continued until exhaustion slowed their punches, until anger ceased to flow from their veins.

He rolled off Marco. They both lay on their backs, staring at the blue sky. If he had been alive, he would be unconscious and bruised for weeks. Instead, while he felt every one of his brother's punches all the way to his soul, none of them left a mark.

At least not a physical one.

Marco rolled to an elbow and stared at him, his fingers flexing and releasing as if he thought of restarting their fight. Luca mirrored his posture and glared.

Marco narrowed his eyes. "She can't see you. I'm doing you a favor."

"Just like you did over a century ago?"

His upper lip curled from his teeth. "I've told you. That *stronzo* lied. He cursed us for no reason."

A lie Marco had told for decades. Words he no longer believed. At first, he hadn't believed Dario Romani, choosing to stand with his brother. But after years of watching Marco, he realized Dario had told the truth when he cursed them into this half life.

He no longer doubted the words Dario had spoken on the day of the curse, but he feared what Marco would do if he appeared to doubt him.

Marco was no longer his beloved older brother. Perhaps he never had been.

He rubbed at the pain in his chest. "He cursed us. And I do not like this state of being."

Marco nodded. "If only we could break the curse."

"You know that will never happen." Except for the ring the woman wore. Did she understand its significance? Did she know she could break his curse?

Did she care?

Either way, he would not share this knowledge with Marco. No telling what his brother would do to the woman. His "welcome" was bad enough.

"I will think on it."

With those words, Marco disappeared. Past history told him his brother wouldn't be back for a while.

Which meant he was free to watch the woman. Yes, she was beautiful. Yes, she wore the ring that could save him. But still. He shouldn't be following her around like a shadow.

He paced across the grass. He should return to his room. Or take a tour of the estate. Anything but give in to the unusual pull tugging him toward the mill, toward the woman.

Releasing a frustrated growl, he stomped toward the woman's apartment. What would it hurt to sit next to her? To listen to what she and the Toscanos had to say? It wasn't being a shadow if he was learning things, right?

Right.

Decision made, he floated through the sturdy wooden door, right into his remodeled office. The woman sat at the table with Maria and Luigi. She was stuffing herself full of Maria's lasagna. Which smelled wonderful. Full of seasoned beef and tomato sauce, the smell transported him back to when he was a child, sitting at his mother's table, eating pasta coated with cheese and ripe tomatoes. He swallowed and shook away the memory. He wished he could taste food instead of staring at it like a salivating dog.

Instead he stared at the ring on her finger as if it would suddenly free him with a thought. It didn't. He sighed and sat in the chair next to her. The woman turned his way, a short smile turning one side of her lips. Her eyes drooped as if she hadn't slept in days. Maybe she'd come here via one of those airplanes. He'd seen the planes flying overhead, read about them in the newspapers, and watched them on the television, but, since he was banished to remain on this property, had never been in one.

"You like the lasagna, Adrianna?" Maria asked. "I made it especially for you."

Adrianna. He liked the sound of her name. Adrianna swallowed her bite, offering Maria a smile.

"I love it. You're the best cook ever."

Judging by her accent, she was not a native Italian but could fluently speak the language. Where was she from?

"Tell us"—Luigi gestured between himself and Maria—"what it's like to be a well-known medium in New York City."

She froze, fork halfway between her plate and her

mouth.

Ah. American. Adrianna was American. He had had never been to America but had read about the country. He would love to visit New York City. If only he could leave this property.

He gave himself a mental smack. *Don't think about it. No if-onlys allowed.*

Wait a minute. Did Luigi just say she was a medium?

****

Adrianna swallowed, stuck the piece of lasagna in her mouth, and chewed. Slowly. Very slowly. The slower the better. Maybe her speed, or lack thereof, would help her come up with something to say.

All too quickly, she finished the mouthful. She had to say something. Both Maria and Luigi were staring at her as if she held all the answers.

Shit.

She placed her fork on her plate and cleared her throat. Then again, for good measure. She could avoid talking about her recent troubles and focus on her early days as a medium when she'd enjoyed taking in clients and talking to spirits. She could do this.

She drew in a deep breath.

"I enjoy helping people." Which was true. Her voice steadied as she continued. "Clients would ask me to help them contact their deceased friend or family. And occasionally get their loved one or a strange apparition to leave them alone. There are a lot of haunted houses in New York City." She twisted her grandfather's ring around her finger, the cool metal and hard stone a calming balm to her pounding heart. "But the fame got to me after a while"—to put it mildly—

"and I decided to leave. I needed a break." She released a breath. She hadn't lied, even if she hadn't told the entire tale.

They appeared fascinated with her brief story. Hopefully they wouldn't ask follow-up questions that started with "why" and ended with "did the fame get to you?"

A puff of air drifted from the chair next to hers. Like before, she turned toward the source. Definitely a ghost. The vague shape hovered around the chair as if the dead person were another guest at dinner. Unlike the earlier pissed-off visitor, this one seemed content to sit and listen, eavesdropping on their conversation. The thing was probably lonely. Most ghosts were. Lonely for human company. Wanting to share their stories before departing this plane. Was this one male or female? The vibe coming off it felt male. With a little concentration she could see his form.

But why bother? She was done with spirits.

She faced the older couple, who now looked at her as if they knew more existed to her story. She sighed. They knew her too well.

Pushing her plate aside, she leaned her elbows on the table. "I hope you don't think I'm rude, but I'm exhausted. Do you mind if I go to bed now?"

"Oh!" Maria stood, reaching for the plate. "We're sorry to keep you up. Of course, you can go to bed. You've had a long day on the plane, and jet lag is awful. I'll clean up and come back tomorrow afternoon. I'll bring you dinner. There's food in the fridge for breakfast and lunch."

Several hugs later, she sagged against the door and drew in a deep breath. Dinner added an extra dose of sleepiness to her existing tiredness. The bed called her name, even if the sky was not fully dark. She yawned, covering her mouth lest the ghost, who still sat at the table, thought her rude.

Gods. Who the hell cared what the damn spook thought? Furthermore, why the hell was it still here?

"You can leave now." She pointed at the window behind the phantom.

And held the point until a rustle of air indicated it had departed the room.

Whew. No problems from that ghost. Unlike the earlier angry spirit. She needed to set up a ward around the apartment to keep the evil one away.

Another yawn stretched her lips as a wave of tiredness encouraged her to forget the spell and fall asleep. Right. As if she'd drift off, leaving herself unprotected from a malevolent entity. She took a step toward the dresser, then paused, chewing on her bottom lip. Would the spell work without candles? All the trappings of a medium remained in her apartment in Brooklyn. She ran a hand through her curls. All she could do was cast the spell minus the candles and hope it worked.

Saying a quick prayer to the gods, she sat in the middle of the room, cast a circle in her mind, and spoke the spell.

Chapter Three

Sunlight streamed through a gap between the wood-paneled shutter and the window, the warm rays waking Adrianna. A wide expanse of plastered ceiling greeted her when she blinked open sleepy eyes. The scent of fresh paint invaded her lungs as she drew in a deep breath. With any luck her time overseas would give her a chance to discover a new career choice. One not involving ghosts. One enabling her to stay in Italy and never return to America.

At least not for anything other than closing her apartment and packing her stuff.

She rolled out of bed and, after a quick bathroom stop, headed toward the window by the door. The same little puff of air she'd felt last night drifted around her. A chill raised goosebumps on her arms.

The ghost.

At least it wasn't the evil entity from yesterday. Either her spell worked, or the creature decided to leave her alone. Thank the gods. This particular one seemed to enjoy watching her. A memory, or maybe it was a dream, crept into her consciousness. Last night. While she slept. A man with short, light brown hair parted on the left and swept to the right had stood by her bed. His clothes, a white shirt unbuttoned at the top with sleeves rolled up and an old-fashioned pair of trousers, dated him to around the beginning of the last century. The details of her dream, or memory, remained sketchy, but she realized this male spirit had watched her sleep.

Great. A stalker spirit.

Which would creep out a normal person, but seeing how she'd spent years talking to ghosts, it only made her curious. Not curious enough to focus on seeing him in the light of day. Nope. She wasn't that curious.

She really needed to stop lying to herself.

Ignoring the ghost, she opened the shutters on the front window, blinking at the bright sunlight. The light always looked brighter in Italy than even the clearest day in the States. Green meadows populated with thick groves of trees spread out from the mill. Her car sat at the end of the drive, across the lawn from the apartment. Through the glass, she heard birds chirping a morning greeting.

She walked to the window behind the table and opened the wooden shutter. More light streamed into the apartment. Across from the window, past the two towers, sat the other wing of the mill. Vines hung from the corners of the collapsed roof, left behind in the cleanup as a rustic touch. Pale brown stones shone in the morning sun, chasing away shadows. Jagged walls ended with stones sticking into the air like claws of a dying beast. Unlike her side of the building, no metal roof covered the wing. The remodelers had yet to make it over to that part of the structure.

The Toscanos had told her structural engineers determined the mill to be safe for exploration. She'd never studied archeology in college, but who didn't dream of exploring ruins and discovering a hidden treasure? Not that she expected a hidden treasure in the ruins of a grain mill, but exploring them was at the top of the day's to-do list.

She twisted her grandfather's ring around, running her fingers over the skin-heated gold, touching the cool, red stone, as she drank in the scenery. Her grandfather used to live in the manor house a couple of miles from the mill until he met her grandmother while they were in college. Although he'd immigrated to America to be with the woman he loved, they returned to Italy every year to visit. A tradition he continued with her once he became her guardian after her grandmother and parents' deaths when she was seven.

She'd spent a lot of time in the manor house when she was a child and missed being able to stay there. Even though she loved the way the ruined mill had been remodeled, it wasn't the same as the home from her memory.

Time to form new memories, Adrianna.

Besides, ghosts filled the manor house. When she was a child, they'd played hide-and-seek together, running up and down the stairs, ducking behind sheet-covered furniture in the attic. And being around ghosts violated her new motto of ignoring the freaky see-through buggers. A motto already broken since some strange male spirit had spent the night with her in the apartment. Was he one she used to play with as a child?

Probably. Maybe that's why he'd watched her all night. Perhaps he remembered her from years ago.

She pinched the bridge of her nose. Did he feel familiar? Like one of her childhood ghostly friends?

Dammit. Was she actually going to use her abilities?

No, no, she was not. She really didn't care.

Right? Right.

The spirit stepped closer. Dammit. She was not dealing with this right now. She did not fly halfway around the world to talk to an Italian ghost. She spun on her heel, marched to the bathroom door, flung it open, and stormed inside, slamming the door shut. As if a closed door would keep a ghost from drifting through the wall.

Gods, could she not go one day without sensing a spirit?

****

Luca paused outside the bathroom door. Since when did he follow women around? While alive, he'd always treated women with respect. And watching one while she slept was the mark of a cad. He knew enough from reading newspapers and watching the television that, although society had changed since his time, shadowing a woman remained an offensive behavior.

Even if he attempted to convince himself watching over her protected her from his brother. Only partially true. Yes, he did not want Marco to harm her, but at the same time, she fascinated him, drawing him into her orbit like a bee to nectar. Was the allure due to her personality and beauty or the ring she wore?

The curse allowed freedom for a price. A selfless act performed for one of Dario Romani's descendants. He remembered the words as if they were spoken moments ago:

For your perfidy, you are cursed into nothingness,
Neither alive nor dead, not of this realm or the next
You will spend eternity on my property, the property you lusted after,
Never to leave it, never to be free
The shadows of your heart will keep you bound to

this land

Cursed you shall be unless you give selflessly to one of my descendants

Only then will you be free

So mote it be.

A flash of light had shot from the red stone of Dario's ring, enveloping Luca in its brightness and ushering him into his present cursed state.

He'd tried several times over the decades to help out the Toscanos. Helping the older, childless couple, though, had no effect on the curse. None. No matter what he did or how many times he tried. Then again, the Toscanos were not direct descendants of Dario's.

But Adrianna was. Or she would not be wearing his ring.

Unless she'd stolen it?

He dismissed the thought as soon as it appeared. Why would she steal Dario's ring, then come to his land with full acceptance and welcome by Luigi and Maria? No, she was not a thief. Then again, he obviously had issues discerning people's characters. Marco had fooled him. For years. Perhaps he could allow himself some slack. Who wanted to think of their family as evil? Even when the proof stood in front of their face.

Yes, Marco had fooled him. But being fooled by his brother was not the same as believing Adrianna wore Dario's ring because she was his descendant. The only logical conclusion was she shared the same blood as Dario.

Which meant she held the possibility of saving him from the curse.

A surge of excitement raced through his veins. Was

he near to being free of this curse? How did one perform a selfless act? Helping Maria and Luigi move furniture and clean the manor house failed to trigger the freeing clause of the curse.

The running water from the bathroom shut off. He swallowed. Time for him to go. Slamming the door in his face was a clear indication she wanted him gone. And yet he stood here while she bathed.

Another shot of excitement zipped through his veins, having nothing to do with freedom and everything to do with the naked woman on the other side of the door.

All he had to do was float through the wood—

Stop it right there, Luca. Get the hell out of here.

After walking through the wooden front door, he strode across the grass and up a rise to the rectangular reflection pool. Two lounge deck chairs faced the mill, and Luca sat in the closest one. Yes, he still technically watched the apartment, but the distance made him less of a shadow.

The things you tell yourself.

"Still watching?"

He jumped as Marco's voice sounded from behind. Dammit. He needed to pay better attention instead of being lost in his thoughts.

Turning, he watched as his brother stepped out of the trees behind the pool.

Don't let him see your interest in Adrianna. Letting a shield of indifference mask his face, he shrugged.

"The reflection of the trees and sky in the pool is relaxing." A truth, but not the reason he sat on the chair. With luck, the redirection would stop Marco from noticing he'd spent the night in Adrianna's room.

Keeping his brother away from her crept to the top of his list of necessities.

Marco strode closer, taking a seat on the other deck chair. "You look deep in thought."

"I am tired of this curse." Another truth. And yet nothing close to his thoughts at the moment.

"There is no way to break it." Marco placed his palms on his thighs and leaned forward. "All of Dario's descendants are dead or no longer visiting this property. We need to forge forward and create our own life."

"How do you propose to do that?" He doubted he could ever accept his life as a spirit. Become used to it, yes, accept it, never.

"Become like me, brother. Think of the living as cursed."

He shook his head, his gaze traveling across the yard, past the blighted stone structure. He would never become like Marco. When they lived, when he still idolized his older brother, he'd wanted to be just like him. Now? Not in the least.

Marco's heavy hand dropped onto his shoulder. He flinched but held his sibling's gaze.

"Brother. You need an adventure. Let's raise the old ones at the mill tonight. We can have a party. Get you out of this funk."

Parties wouldn't help his mood. Only being freed from the curse would cheer him up. But if throwing a party would draw his brother's attention away from Adrianna and her apartment, he could attend a party and act like he enjoyed it.

Sticking on what he hoped was a convincing smile, he nodded. "All right, then. Let's have a party."

****

After a quick breakfast of cheese and Maria's homemade bread, Adrianna changed into shorts and a T-shirt to explore the ruins. Maria had left a photo album of the mill's discovery and subsequent restoration. When first discovered, vines covered the stone walls, and trees thrust from between cracks in the mortar to loom over the two towers bracketing the mill's entrance. As cleanup progressed and large piles of vegetation were removed, tunnels were discovered under the walls. Fallen rocks were repaired or replaced, turning the ruin into a place of beauty.

She stepped outside the apartment with the flashlight in hand and turned from left to right to take in the scenery. Amazing what one could miss seeing when tired.

To her left was the dilapidated wing waiting to be remodeled. To her right, up a short grass-covered hill, was a swimming pool. Rectangular, with a half deck composed of red tiles, it doubled as a deep reflection pool. She could hardly wait to swim in it this afternoon. Behind the pool were stairs framed by two carved columns with an arch leading to the top of a hill. Pretty and definitely worth exploring, but first she wanted to look around the sixteenth-century structure.

Age crept from the stones. If she concentrated, she could see the workers walking around, going about their business. Centuries of workers and farmers bringing their grain to the mill to grind. Not ghosts, more like auras frozen in time giving glimpses of the past but with no chance of communicating with her.

She refused to concentrate.

Although, she had to admit, she wanted to see the ghost who'd visited her last night. The one from her dream. The one who'd watched her sleep, then left while she showered. A shiver rippled across her skin.

How many spirits haunted this place? Since arriving, she had counted two. Were there more, watching from a distance, not interfering with the living? Or were there others like the demonic entity, hellbent on frightening anyone who dared set foot on their territory?

Great. She really couldn't get away from ghosts despite trying hard to ignore them.

Shoving her gods-given abilities into a dark hole was impossible and foolish. She was a medium no matter what she wanted, and the sooner she accepted that fact, the better.

Her heart pounded a skittish dance. She drew in several deep breaths. One of these days. Today was not that day. Today she wanted to explore the ruins. Soak in the sun. Swim.

Ruins first.

Birds chirped as they hopped from tree to tree, rustling the leaves. A gentle breeze played through her hair. The quiet calmed her heart, her mind, as peace crept into her soul. No telling how long it would take for all the stress of the Big Apple to leave. Getting over her failure would take even longer. If ever.

She sighed. Enough thinking on the past. What was done was done. No changes. No do-overs. Only moving forward.

She walked to the unrenovated wing, climbed through a cutout in the stone, and began exploring. Damp air overlaid with the odor of rotting vegetation filled her nose. Humidity wrapped around her like a tightening shawl. Parts of the roof remained intact, allowing sunlight to dapple moss-covered walls, leaving other places in darkness. Some areas she refused to enter—those inky, black expanses of stone walls where a steady dripping of water echoed in the dark space. Her flashlight picked out potholes in the floor, dropping to who knew where. The light could not penetrate to the bottom. Nope, while she was excited to explore the ruins, it wasn't worth it to trip over a pile of rocks or break a leg falling into a hole. She kept to the lit places, which were hard enough to navigate.

As seen in Maria's pictures, tunnels led under the building, dark passages to nowhere. A shudder racked her limbs. The beam from the flashlight barely scratched the inky blackness. No way was she exploring those creepy channels by herself.

Another area had a large arch with a flight of stairs leading down to a tunnel. Her vision dimmed as she stared at the stone steps. A fuzzy picture came into focus in her mind. Shadows moved against the backdrop of a light. Stringed music swelled into a symphony of sound. Someone waited in the shadows. Waited for her. In her premonition she walked down those stairs, walking toward…whom? The man remained hidden, outside the view of her vision.

She blinked, and the vision vanished. Damn premonitions. Always teasing, never showing.

Prickles spread across her scalp, falling in waves down her spine. She'd seen too many spirits in her life to be scared of them, but their nearness often gave her chills. Not a true fear reaction, more like a caution, a warning to respect otherworldly creatures.

The same caution she now felt standing outside the archway leading to the dark tunnel. Something lurked down there in the darkness, deep inside the bowels of the ruins. Something not living. Something she both wanted to see and avoid.

What would happen if she entered? If she walked down those stairs, passed through the archway, strode into the tunnel? Would she return? Or would she be lost forever?

Get a grip, Adrianna. Where the hell did all those thoughts come from? Sure, the mill was creepier on the inside than it looked like from the outside, but still. The pitch-black passageway was only a tunnel. At one point in time, she assumed, water had rushed through it. Nothing to fear.

Self-talk failed to stop another set of chills from crawling across her flesh. Maybe she should move on from the tunnel. Explore someplace else. Let whatever lay hidden stay obscured.

Chapter Four

Luca walked among the other spirits at Marco's party. Held in a cavernous underground room below the mill, the parties consisted of local ghosts who flew in for the occasion. Unlike him and his brother, these ghosts weren't confined to one location. They could travel across the country if they wanted, although they remained strongest near their places of life and death. Several of them had been musicians and came to play in the orchestra or string quartet, depending on how many of them appeared. Music filled the room, the stringed instruments part of the magical illusion. Not only were the parties a gathering place for the ghosts, but they served the larger purpose of providing a tactile experience. Touch was rare for non-corporeal beings. Missed.

Spirits would do almost anything to run fingers over flesh without the person running away screaming.

Hence the large attendance at these parties. Somehow Marco created an illusion allowing all who came to become corporeal. Luca was powerful enough to create small items to decorate his personal room, but the skill had taken decades to perfect and was nothing on the scale of his brother's galas. He had never attempted to give a ghost a physical body. How Marco found the massive amount of energy needed to manifest bodies for multiple ghosts remained a mystery.

Yet another subject Marco refused to tell him about. The tight-lipped bastard.

His brother always seemed to know when Luca became focused on issues Marco preferred to avoid. As a distraction, Marco would throw a party under the guise of making him happy—as if that would ever happen while in this damned half life. If he didn't know better, he'd think his brother read his mind and discovered he no longer believed his lies.

Over the years, he'd become adept at fooling his brother. Pretending he still believed and idolized him. Feigning enjoyment of his new life.

But he could not lie to himself. He hated being a ghost.

And now he had his chance for redemption.

Once he figured out how to convince Adrianna to help him. First, he needed for her to see him. But how?

"Luca!" Giorgia waved at him from a crowd of gossiping women.

He returned the wave, waiting as she hurried to him, leaving her companions to their giggles and conspiratorial glances.

"Good evening, Giorgia. How are you this evening?" Luca gave the buxom older woman a hug.

She took a step away, slapping him on the arm with her folded fan. "Look at you! All dressed up!"

He rubbed at his arm where her fan landed. Not a hard hit, but it never ceased to amaze him how real things felt or how the guests at these parties seemed to come alive. His grin stuck on his lips at her usual greeting. "Of course. It's a party."

"A ball. It's a ball, not a party."

"As you wish." He gave her a little bow. "You look

dashing yourself. Nice dress."

It was the same dress she always wore. Stuck in her time period of late 1800s, Giorgia repeated the same lines every time he saw her, as if she could not progress past her point of death. Maybe she couldn't. Others here were the same. Their words consistent from one party—ball—to the next.

"Aren't you the kind gentleman? Well, well, you must go dance with the younger ladies, and I need to return to my friends."

Her gown flared around her ankles as she turned to walk back to the circle of female ghosts.

His gaze followed her as he smiled at her circle of friends. They giggled, a few holding their fans over their lips.

Outside of this place, they reverted back to ethereal beings, able to touch items only if they concentrated. While he and Marco had always been able to touch each other, the other unliving could only do so at these gatherings.

No wonder the parties brought in ghosts from all over the region. Marco's trick allowed them to remain as strong as when they haunted their homes as well as regain physicality.

He'd enjoyed the parties too. Enjoyed the women. Enjoyed touching someone, anyone, other than his brother. Until he'd realized his brother wasn't throwing galas to be nice to other spirits or even him. No, Marco threw the parties to distract him and gain strength. Somehow, gathering a group of ghosts together fueled Marco's power.

Unfortunately, he had yet to discover the secret. Asking only led to a smirk. Or a shake of the head. Or a plain, annoying "no."

Perhaps he'd never learn the answer.

Did it really matter? The only thing he cared about was reversing the curse and freeing himself. And Marco.

He stopped walking and rubbed his forehead. Maybe not Marco. His brother seemed more interested in remaining a cursed creature than being freed.

With the way Marco acted, Luca doubted his brother could ever perform a selfless deed to break the curse.

But he would find a reversal to the curse. He had to. No other option existed. Well, no other appealing option. Sure, he could remain in this half life state, attending parties at night, floating around the estate during the day, becoming more irritated with his brother as the years passed.

No. He would not live this way anymore. Adrianna was his way out of here. Provided she wanted to help free him.

But for now, he wanted to get to know her. To have her know him. Wishful thinking on his part.

How was he supposed to talk to her?

He twisted out of the way of a couple walking arm in arm, their eyes only for each other. He apologized to the man he bumped. Wandering through a crowd while lost in thought only led to running into others. He needed to concentrate on the problem. He needed to discover how to communicate with Adrianna.

Wait a minute. She definitely sensed his presence, but could she see him? Luigi had mentioned she was a medium. But mediums came in different shades. Some could see ghosts. Some could only sense them. Some could actually interact. Which kind was she?

Only one way to find out. He had to try to talk to her instead of just watching her.

He stepped around the long table containing a silver punch bowl filled with a pink liquid none of the attendees drank. Appearances were everything even in death. And a ball needed a bowl of punch. Functionality be damned.

He glanced around the room, looking for Marco. No sense in his brother catching on to his plans. He needed to ensure the man left with one of his paramours before he tried to talk to Adrianna.

Distracting him and gaining power weren't the only reasons Marco threw the parties.

"Have you seen my brother?" he asked one of the guests.

The man shook his head. "Not for some time. He left with Lydia, and I haven't seen him since."

He squeezed the man's shoulder before continuing around the room. Three more people told him the same thing. No Marco. Based on past experience, Marco would remain occupied until dawn when the partygoers returned to their homes. While he and his brother walked in the daylight, they were the exception to the rule. Most ghosts either hid during the day or remained in dark corners of the homes they haunted.

Assured Marco's departure meant he would not return to the party the rest of the night, Luca walked out of the entrance to the ballroom and into the long tunnel. Halfway through the tunnel, he became non-corporeal once again. A small landing sat at the tunnel exit. A flight of stairs led upward through a columned arch. He jogged up the stairs, dim light from the half-moon casting elongated shadows across the grass, gnarled claws reaching toward the apartment.

He stopped at the edge of the mill across from the apartment where Adrianna slept. The glass window faced him like a dark mirror. How should he approach? Over a century had passed since he had spoken with a living woman. How did men greet women in this century? He saw multiple examples on television throughout the years, some of them awkward.

And none of them applicable in this situation.

Should he knock on the door? Or walk through the wall? She'd told him to leave her room last night. Perhaps he could manifest outside of the party. Would she be able to see him if he concentrated hard enough?

Madonna help him.

For the first time in decades, She did. Adrianna stood in the window.

****

Flickering lights woke Adrianna from a deep sleep. Her heart pounded like a drumline, quick staccato beats sending a jolt of adrenaline racing along tensed nerves. She froze, lying on her side, listening as a soft vibration shook her bones. What was happening? Low voices punctuated with laughter circled around the room. Thin whispers of music drifted in through the windows. What the hell? Was she dreaming? Or were trespassing thrill seekers exploring the ruins in the middle of the night? If that was the case, she needed to kick ass and take names. She rubbed her head. Right. She should dial 113 and let the *Polizia Municipale* handle it.

She reached for her phone, then put it back on the nightstand as the melody turned into the stringed notes of Beethoven. Beethoven? The music sounded like a chamber orchestra. Since when did trespassers out for a thrill bring along violins and cellos? Was someone pranking her?

She rolled out of bed and strode to the window, yanking on her thin summer robe as she walked. Maybe she should close the shutters and pretend an orchestra hadn't taken up residence in the ruins. Glimmering lights drew her attention to the opposite wing of the mill where a man stood staring at her window. At her. Breath caught in her lungs as she froze.

But only for a brief moment until she realized it wasn't a man, at least not a living one. Her breath escaped on a whoosh of relief. Intuition whispered the man was the spirit who'd watched her last night.

The one from her dream.

Shadows clung to his body, ghostly fingers releasing as he stepped into the dim slash of moonlight. Lights flickered from behind him, like the dying gasps of sputtering candles. Dressed in a white shirt with an old-fashioned high collar, sleeves rolled halfway up his forearms, and dark trousers, he reminded her of a working man in a World War I photograph. As if he had removed his coat and tie and rolled up his sleeves to get to work.

Except the men in those photos didn't sport the wide-eyed, happy look of this man. Ghost. Whatever. Yeah, he wasn't the only one surprised. She'd sworn to never see a ghost again, yet there stood a ghost, captured by her gaze. The man was hot, in an old-fashioned way. At least he didn't sport a handle-bar moustache.

He gestured to her, his hand beckoning in a "come here" motion.

She squeezed the bridge of her nose. Was she actually thinking of heading his way? Judging by the way her feet pointed toward the door, she'd already decided. Dammit. She might not want to see a ghost or speak to a spirit, but past experience told her if she ignored them, they ramped up the annoying factor.

How bad could it be to talk to an attractive spirit?

Decision made, she tightened the belt of her robe, stuck her feet in her flip-flops, and headed out the door. The soft *flip-flop-flip* of her shoes on the grass was lost in the strings of Beethoven drifting from the tunnels.

The man watched her approach. He gave a little nod as she stopped in front of him, his half smile mirroring hers.

Up close, he exuded an aura she'd never felt from a ghost. He felt alive to her internal senses.

Which was ridiculous. Clearly, he was not alive. She saw brown stones through his body. Not a typical characteristic of the living.

She wiped her palms on the sides of her robe. "Hello. I'm Adrianna Sinclair. Who are you?"

His grin grew. "I am Luca Fausto. It is nice to meet you."

"It's nice to meet you too." Her head tilted. "You stayed with me last night, didn't you?"

He winced, rubbing the back of his neck. "I wanted to ensure you were all right."

Interesting. A protective ghost. "From the evil spirit?"

He shoved his hands in his pockets. "You are from America, yes?"

Okay, then. Her protective ghost clearly had some sort of an issue with the malevolent spirit he refused to discuss. She'd give him a pass.

For now.

"Yep. I'm from New York City. Where are you from?"

The grin disappeared as his eyes grew shaded. Uh-oh. The normally calming getting-to-know-you question struck a nerve.

"I live here now." His flat voice wrapped around her with threads of anger.

Anger? Was he upset because he'd died, or did he really dislike the mill that much? And if it was the mill, what about it caused his reaction?

"In the mill?"

He nodded. Glanced down at the arched stairway and back to her. "Would you like to see?"

She wiped her palms on her robe as she stared at the forbidding tunnel. Her heart picked up its pace, pounding a warning. She swallowed.

What was the harm in going down a flight of stairs into a dark tunnel with an attractive ghost?

Right. Was she actually asking that question? The horror of Ted Bundy popped into her mind. Her eyes narrowed on Luca. Dollars to doughnuts the noises coming from the tunnel belonged to ghosts. While evil spirits could harm an unsuspecting living person, or even a suspecting one, she was prepared to battle the thing.

She hoped.

A burst of laughter exploded from the tunnel. She might have sworn off ghosts, but seeing a group of them together was a chance she couldn't pass up.

Her gaze relaxed as she offered Luca a smile. *Oh come on, Adrianna, stop lying to yourself. You really want to spend the evening with the smoking-hot ghost.*

"I'd love to."

The hopeful expression on his face brightened. He held out his hand for a second before pressing his lips together. With a slight shake of his head, he swept his hand away from her and gestured down the stairs toward the tunnel. "Come."

He started forward, and like in her premonition, she followed, ignoring the creepy feeling the tunnel exuded. Earlier in the day the feeling spooked her, turning her away from its stygian depths. Now she headed straight into the belly of the ruin. Clearly there was something wrong with her.

Halfway through the tunnel, the air grew lighter as if she passed through the perimeter of a ward. Perhaps a spell existed to warn away the living, to separate the dead from the rest of the world. Whatever the reason, the scary feeling dissipated, vanishing into the solid stone wall.

Luca grabbed her hand. She gasped. The fact Luca—a ghost—grasped her hand caused her heart to skip a beat. He touched her, but not in the typical way of ghosts where their hand or body passed through hers as they tried, yet failed, to make physical contact. No, he touched her like a living man. Skin on skin. Warm skin on her suddenly damp palm.

The world around her faded until only Luca remained. Her wide gaze met his, and he smiled. She tightened her hand around his, lacing their fingers together. How was this possible? In all her years of talking to the otherworldly creatures, she'd never held hands with one. When a ghost touched her—or tried to touch her—a cold feeling would ripple across her body.

Not now. Now the touch of his warm palm sent a totally different type of tingle through her body. The tingle a woman got from touching a man she wanted.

Which was crazy on so many levels she wouldn't even bother to count.

Instead, she decided to go with it, to see what he wanted. Ghosts always wanted something. At least in her experience. Acknowledging one spirit—or even touching him for that matter—wouldn't mess up her swearing off the creatures.

Right? Right.

"How can you touch me?"

A grin spread across his lips. "It's a secret."

One she needed to learn. No other ghost she'd met possessed that ability. How was it even possible for a spirit to turn corporeal?

Lights grew brighter and the chamber music louder the farther they walked. They stepped into a huge room, and she gasped. For more reasons than one.

Instead of the expected underground cavern hewed from stone, they stepped into a ballroom. A large, crystal, four-tiered chandelier hung from the ceiling, tiny candles illuminating the place with an ethereal glow. Paintings in gold frames interspersed with flickering candles in sconces covered the two-story-tall walls. Shimmering sparks of light reflected off the golden frames and spun around the room. Artfully arranged swaths of tapestries lined the back from ceiling to floor as if they concealed stone walls or passages. Light from an unseen source lit the top of the room, turning it into a painted ceiling.

And that wasn't the amazing part. Well, okay, the grandeur of the room was pretty amazing, but not nearly as interesting as the hundreds of spirits dancing in period gowns and tailed tuxes.

Their outfits ran the gamut from sixteenth century to the early twentieth century. A variety of colors and styles swirled on the dance floor as the ghosts bent and swayed in time to the music.

A row of musicians sat on a raised platform to the left of the dance floor, playing violins, violas, and cellos. The men stared intently at sheet music set on fragile metal stands. Old-fashioned cushioned chairs and fainting couches lined the walls, along with a long table containing what appeared to be refreshments.

Spirits gathered in small groups, laughing and talking and gesturing toward others. A ghost party. She was at a ghost party. She was surrounded by ghosts wearing formal clothes.

Which was different, to say the least. All ones who visited her before had worn the clothing they died in. It wasn't like a ghost could go shopping at Ghost-Mart and pick out a ball gown.

And yet somehow the impossible happened.

A brush of fabric against her legs snapped her attention from the room full of spirits to her lower body. She froze in place, staring at her new outfit. What the hell? Instead of her PJs and robe, she wore a ball gown. A beautiful blue ball gown. Smooth fabric rubbed between her fingers as she lifted the skirt. Instead of flip-flops, ballet-like slippers graced her feet. Her breath hitched as she turned to Luca. He now wore a black tux with tails, a waistcoat, and white shirt with a bow tie. *Seriously. What. The. Hell?*

"Do you like the gown?" He squeezed her hand. "I can change it if you prefer a different one."

"You dressed me?" She shut her gaping mouth and lowered her voice. How was it even possible to create her a ball gown? Creating period dress for spirits she could somewhat understand. But creating illusionary clothing for a living person?

What other magical skills did he have?

A wrinkle formed between his brows. "This bothers you?"

Yes. "No, no. I'm just surprised. Did you dress all of them?" She gestured to the room with her free hand.

His jaw tensed, the muscle flexing and releasing. "No. Only you."

"Then how—?"

"Do you want to walk around? There is punch."

Okay, then. No conversation about the secret of clothing phantoms. At least not tonight.

Wait a minute. Did he say punch was available?

"Punch? Can you drink punch?"

He shook his head. "No, none of us can. However, a party isn't a party without punch. When we throw a party, punch is always provided. No one drinks, but everyone likes the punch bowl and cups on the table."

In an odd way, it made sense. People hung on to the trappings of life even in death.

"Are you sure I can drink it?" The bigger question being did she dare?

He stared at the long table as one side of his lips twisted. "Maybe not. My apologies for offering."

Illusions. Everything here was illusionary. Despite the deception and the close presence of hundreds of ghosts, she loved what she saw. Being transported through time while remaining in the present was a little strange but in a nice type of way. The relaxing music soothed the frayed edges of her soul.

She glanced at Luca, her gaze traveling down his arm to their joined hands. Was he an illusion too?

A question for later. Tonight, she wanted to enjoy attending a ball with an attractive man. Tomorrow, she would get answers.

Her fingers tightened. Watching the dead dance and interact with each other like they had when alive was unbelievable.

Yeah, she liked this place. Even if it meant spending the evening surrounded by hundreds of ghosts.

A couple walked past them to the dance floor, the woman's gown swaying in time to their steps. She turned her gaze to Luca. What would it be like to dance with him? To be held by a ghost?

"Want to dance?"

His eyes widened. "You know these dances?"

"I took ballroom dance lessons." For three months. "The steps don't seem much different." And even if they were, she wasn't about to pass up a chance to dance with a crowd of ghosts. How many mediums could say they had done that?

She met his gaze, holding it as a current sparked between them. A current sizzling with promise.

Forsaking all ghostly interactions no longer seemed like a valid response to her making a fatal mistake with a client.

A grin curved his lips as if he knew her dance skills lacked finesse. "I will show you."

He led her to the dance floor, pulled her close, but not so close their bodies touched, and whirled her into a waltz. His dance skills far outweighed her own, despite her lessons.

She met his gaze. Crinkles spread from the corners of his eyes as if he laughed a lot or spent all his days in the sun. His large hand rested against her waist as he led her through the dance steps. Warmth spread outward from his touch, pooling lower and turning her legs into a quivering pile of noodles. She stumbled.

Damn it. Talk about embarrassing.

He pulled her closer, keeping her on her feet. Okay, then. Maybe stumbling a dance step wasn't as embarrassing as she feared. She enjoyed his touch, the feel of his hand upon her waist, the way his other palm tightened on hers. His gaze penetrated hers as if he saw into her innermost being. Instead of feeling naked, a warm glow pulsed through her veins. She could stay in his arms forever.

A couple brushed against them, snapping her out of her languid trance. Her gaze drifted around the ballroom. The ghosts still danced, turning in time to the music, but several of them shot her startled glances as if they recognized her as a living, breathing being. But since they focused more on their partners or their friends than her, she ignored them.

Curious ghosts lacked the scare factor of evil spirits. They probably wondered why a living person invaded their ball.

"Can they tell I'm alive?"

Luca shrugged as he twirled her around. "Maybe. Maybe not. I do not know."

"You've never brought another living person to one of these parties?"

"Never."

"So I'm your first?"

He blinked, then grinned as a tint of red flushed across his cheeks. "In a manner of speaking, yes."

Time to stop with the mild innuendos. Dancing with him seemed so real she forgot for a moment he had probably lived in a time when women were not encouraged to express their sexuality.

"You're a very good dancer."

He dipped his head. "Thank you. You aren't bad either."

Not bad wasn't exactly a ringing endorsement of her dance skills. At least she could keep up with him without stepping on his toes. Always a plus.

"How long have you lived at the mill?"

The grin slid from his lips. "Too long."

"What is the definition of too long?"

A heavy sigh weighted the air between them. "Since 1910."

About the time period she'd thought based on his clothing. Judging from his expression, he had not accepted his death. Like many other spirits she had helped over the years.

But the thought of helping him pass to the other side left a small hard ball bouncing around inside her stomach. She wanted him to stay on this side with her.

Gah. She'd been through a long, dry spell with men, but still. No way could she be falling for a man she'd just met. No, not even a man, a ghost.

Giving herself a mental smack, she focused on their conversation.

"I'm sorry. Did you die in an accident at the mill?"

"In a manner of speaking." His gaze cut to the side for a second. "What about you? What brings you to Italy?"

Interesting. He wanted to avoid the topic of his death. Was he ashamed? Still mad about the accident that had stolen his life? Or was it something more sinister? Most stable, non-evil spirits she'd helped enjoyed talking about themselves. Most people did. Psychology played a large part in being a medium.

Except for when using the skill failed. Like when the medium ignored obvious clues and gave her client wrong advice which led to the client's death.

What do you know? It looked like she and Luca had something in common. Neither wanted to speak of their past.

But she had to answer his question. Judging by the look on his face, she'd already taken too long to respond.

She drew in a slow breath and released it with a rush of air. "My grandfather used to live in the manor house. The one they sold before discovering the mill ruins?"

He nodded as if he knew about the place. Which he probably did since the mill was a few miles from the large house.

"Anyway, my grandfather raised me after my parents died when I was seven. His wife died the same year, so it was just him and me. Every summer he'd bring me Italy, to the manor house. He wanted me to learn about my family. To see where our family used to live. We owned all this property. Still own the vineyards and farming lands. When I got tired of the fast-paced life in New York City, I decided to come back here. I've stayed in touch with Maria and Luigi, and they encouraged me to return."

There. She managed to tell the truth while

detouring around the real issue causing her to leave New York.

His eyes narrowed. "I seem to remember a small child running around the manor house in the summers a couple of decades ago. That was you?"

Her heart fluttered. "Were you one of the ghosts I used to play with?"

He shook his head. "No."

Interesting. So much for thinking he'd watched over her last night because he remembered playing hide-and-seek with her as a child.

The music stopped, and the dancers turned and applauded for the musicians. Luca released her but remained close. Her fingers tingled to touch him again. The small distance between them left her aching to close the gap.

"Do you want to dance the next dance or relax in a chair?" He gestured to the row of half-occupied chairs lining the wall.

Being held by him or leaning against the wall? Her grandfather didn't raise a fool.

She smiled as she stared into his eyes. "I'll take another dance."

A gleam lit his hazel irises as he grasped her hand and led her into the dance. Yep, she definitely made the right decision. He wanted to hold her as much as she wanted to be held. Tingles swept through her veins as he pulled her a little closer than the last dance. Still a respectable distance, but close enough to feel the heat from his body.

Another "how was that possible" question she'd focus on tomorrow.

"So you own the Romani property?"

"It's a joint ownership between me and a couple of distant cousins. My grandfather had two older siblings, a brother and a sister, but the sister became a nun and died in a convent about ten years or so after World War II, and his brother only had one child. Just like my grandfather. That son had a couple of kids, and those are the cousins who share ownership of the estate with me." She shrugged. "I haven't seen my cousins in years. We talk mainly through email."

His brows drew together. "Email?"

Oh, right. He'd died in 1910. Long before the advent of All Things Computer.

"Electronic mail? It goes over the internet?"

A vee formed between his brows. "I have read of this internet but do not understand how so much information can be on an invisible web. Is it like a spider's web?"

"Not exactly. I can try to explain it to you some other time if you want." She wasn't going to discuss technology when she could focus on dancing with a man—a ghost, even if he currently had solid characteristics—who sent tingles of excitement through her veins. A ghost. A ghost who turned her on.

Who would've thought? And not just Luca. This entire evening fell under the unbelievable category, from the solid dancing ghosts, to the magic of a ballroom, to the corporeal and totally hot ghost who held her in his arms. No one would believe her if she tried to explain. Not even her fellow psychic friends.

Trying to understand everything happening made her mind spin. Or maybe the warm touch of Luca's hand on her back was the cause. After each dance, he pulled her a little closer, until their bodies brushed against each other. A soft thrill of excitement spread through her blood.

They stayed on the floor for several more dances, as close as possible while gazing into each other's eyes, their conversation light. Her feet hurt, her dry throat needed a large glass of water—illusionary punch wouldn't cut it—but she refused to tell Luca she needed a break. Who was she fooling? She enjoyed being in his arms too much to stop. Her last boyfriend had been several years ago, and taking random lovers never appealed to her. So yeah, a very long dry spell.

It wouldn't kill her to wait for a much-needed glass of water.

Luca spun her in a circle, whirling her around at the same time chimes sounded. He pulled her close, stopping on the middle of the dance floor. Just as she started to ask what was wrong, the musicians set down their instruments and stood.

Ding-dong-ding! Another round of chimes filled the air. A shiver spread from him into her as his grip tightened on her hand and waist.

What the hell was wrong?

A low shuffle of hundreds of footsteps echoed in the cavernous room as everyone walked in quiet clusters to the tunnel entrance. Instead of the gossiping titters and low rumbling laughter of the party, only the shuffle of shoes against the wooden floor filled the air.

"What's going on?"

Cocking his head to the side, he pressed his lips together. "Party is over. We need to leave."

Her gaze cut to the silent spirits waiting to leave. No pushing. No yelling. Eerie silence surrounded them as they waited in line to exit. Since when did ghosts leave in an orderly manner instead of zipping away through the walls?

"Why are they all going out the same way? Why not go through the walls and ceiling?"

"They cannot. The only way to leave the party is through the tunnel." His gaze darted from the back of the room to the ceiling. Tension etched his voice. "Come. We cannot be here when the illusion fades."

"What happens?" Would the room collapse?

While the spirits didn't appear afraid, they also didn't linger, as if their role in a play had ended and they needed to exit the stage.

He shook his head at her question, grabbed her hand, and led her to the exit line. "Hurry."

"What happens?"

"I don't want you here when the time ends."

Maybe her ball gown would vanish, and the spirits would definitely realize she lived. Or maybe a living person could not be present and unharmed when the illusion fell. Whatever the reason, his sense of urgency hurried her forward.

The slow procession stepped into the tunnel in pairs. Adrianna lost track of them once they stepped into the darkness. When it was their turn to leave, she glanced at the ballroom. Would she see it again?

A slight flicker occurred at the back of the room, like a lightbulb burning out, and the illusion of tapestries morphed into stone and back to fabric. Her breath hitched.

Luca tugged her hand, and she stepped into the tunnel, leaving behind the fading magic.

Once in the tunnel, the warmth of his palm faded, turning into the cold touch of an otherworldly creature.

Her dress faded into nothing, leaving her in her pajamas, robe, and flip-flops. As soon as they passed up the stairs and through the archway, the spirits vanished into the shadows, once again transparent ghosts.

She and Luca passed under the archway and headed toward her apartment. Dawn lit the horizon, pinks and oranges spreading across the sky in a dance of glory. Dawn? Was it already morning?

Luca walked beside her to the apartment like a protector, his head turning a little from side to side as if ensuring nothing attacked. Was he worried? Or was this his normal behavior?

"Open the door to your apartment now." He glanced over his shoulder while she grabbed the doorknob. "Good night, Adrianna."

She pushed open the door, looking behind her to the night shadows spread across the lawn. Was something out there? At least the wards around her apartment would hold against evil for several more days.

She hoped.

Once she stepped inside, he held out his hand, palm up. She rested her hand on top of his, pausing midair since his physical form no longer existed. He bent over her hand, brushing his lips across her knuckles. A cold chill ran up her arm.

"Until we meet again."

"Thank you for the lovely evening, Luca."

"You are most welcome." He glanced over his shoulder. "Now go inside and close the door." When she paused, he gestured in a go-away motion. "Go on now. Close the door."

Lest she upset him, she obeyed, shutting the door

in his face. She counted to three and opened it. No Luca. No noise drifted from the tunnel. No lights flickered besides the breaking dawn. She stuck her head out the door, looking left and right. Because ghosts always walked away instead of vanishing on a thought. Right. Like she was going to see him hightailing it to his car.

She closed the door and locked it. Locks wouldn't keep out the supernatural, but human trespassers were a possibility. Years of living in a big city instilled habits.

Had she truly spent the night with a ghost at a party attended by a ballroom full of spirits? She closed the shutters, placed her robe on a chair, and crawled into bed. Pulling the covers up, she shook her head. So much for ignoring her medium abilities and paying no attention to ghosts. Unless she'd dreamed the whole thing, then sleepwalked outside to the gravel-filled patio area.

A possibility. She used to sleepwalk as a child. After her parents died. Until her grandfather took her to a child psychiatrist. Over twenty years without a sleepwalking incident and it suddenly happened again?

Stranger things had happened.

Chapter Five

A knock on her door jerked Adrianna awake. Where…what…oh, right. Italy. The mill. She drew in a deep breath of air laced with the smell of fresh paint. The knock sounded again, louder this time. Why was someone knocking in the morning? She glanced at her phone, eyes widening. Three thirty in the afternoon. She'd slept the day away.

"Adrianna!" Maria's voice was punctuated by her knocking.

"Just a minute!" She grabbed her robe and hurried to the door. Yanking it open, she offered Maria an apologetic grin. "So sorry."

Maria looked her up and down, lips pressed. "Are you sick? You're still in your night clothes."

She stepped back, holding the door open. Should she tell Maria what happened last night? Had it been a dream or reality? It sure as hell had felt real. Maria stepped inside, carrying a food container. Adrianna's stomach growled, reminding her of her lack of meals since last evening. She slapped a hand over her belly as if that would stop its rumblings.

Maria set the food on the counter in the kitchenette and shot her a "spill the beans" expression. Had it been a dream or reality? She decided to go with dream. If her psychic friends wouldn't believe what she saw, what made her think Maria would?

"I had a weird dream. I thought there were trespassers exploring the ruins, but then I realized it was ghosts. They were having a party. You know, an old-fashioned ball, long dresses and everything. I danced all night and apparently slept all day."

Maria tilted her head to the side, her gaze a penetrating laser. "You saw the ghosts?"

"You believe what I saw was real?"

Maria rolled her eyes. "Of course. You can't visit this place without hearing about the ghosts. Like that one the other night." She crossed herself. "You didn't see that bad one again, did you?"

She shook her head. "No, thank goodness."

"Good. This place feels like many ghosts live here. You know what I mean." Another eye roll. "Of course, you do. You're the medium."

"You need to tell potential renters the place is haunted. That will keep away those who are bothered by the thought of otherworldly creatures and bring in those who love paranormal experiences. Ghost walks and spending the night in haunted hotels are all the rage in the States."

"Truly?" Maria's brows rose. "We were afraid if we mentioned it no one would come."

"Include it with your description on the internet. People will love it."

"Hmm. We'll think on it." She walked to the door, pausing with her hand on the knob. "I've made you dinner, but Luigi and I have plans and cannot eat with you tonight."

"I'll miss seeing you."

"And we'll miss seeing you too. But we have mass and choir rehearsal, and we can't miss it. I'll come tomorrow for dinner, okay?"

"Sounds good." Questions rushed through her mind as Maria opened the door. She should have asked them earlier, but no one ever accused her of thinking straight first thing upon waking. "Hey, I meant to ask you the other night about all those stories about the mill."

Maria raised a brow. "What about them?"

"What were they?" Did any of them have to do with Luca?

Maria narrowed her eyes. One hand dashed back and forth through the air. "You know. Our land had a mill where grain was ground. Then industrialization took over. The mill was shut down and lost to history. It happens around the country. We aren't the only place where the location of an old mill was lost. Except ours was closed due to an earthquake and loss of lives." A gleam sparked her eyes, making her appear years younger. "When I was a girl, I imagined the earth swallowing the place and all the people in it, and I was the one to find it and show it to the world." She snorted a laugh. "I found it all right, but not in the fantasy way I dreamed about."

Adrianna smiled at Maria's childhood dreams. "So nothing about ghosts?"

"Are you worried that evil one will return?"

Yes. "Not really. My dream made me wonder if you'd heard stories about why the mill was haunted."

Maria shrugged. "This property has been around for centuries. It's not surprising if a ghost or three reside here. You're the medium. You know more about these things than I do."

Was the older woman hiding something? Or did she really not know any stories about why Luca lived here? Whatever the answer, Maria had stepped out on the patio, ending the conversation.

Well, there was always tomorrow.

Adrianna followed her outside, giving her a hug. "See you tomorrow, Maria."

She stood at the door, watching until Maria drove off, her car disappearing behind a strand of trees.

She closed the door and leaned against it. Had last night really happened? Or had it all been a dream? No, she knew better. She'd really spent an entire evening in the arms of a hot ghost, dancing waltzes played by spirit musicians. In the light of day, knowing and believing separated into two different ideas. Those divergent beliefs needed to be reconciled. Sooner rather than later.

She pressed her fingers against the bridge of her nose and dug in a little, the pain snapping her focus to last night. *Admit it, Adrianna, you danced with a ghost. You spent the evening in the arms of a dead man.*

Well, put like that, it sounded more disgusting than romantic. Last night had been one of the best nights of her life. Despite being in the presence of spirits. Not all spirits were bad. Allowing herself to interact with them like she always had throughout her life had nothing to do with her mistake, her failure.

Still. The less she talked to them the better. Right?

As the question hung in the air unanswered, she shook her head. Okay. No sense lying to herself. She enjoyed talking to Luca and wanted to see him again. Would another party be thrown tonight? Would she be invited?

How did he throw the party? How did non-corporeal creatures become corporeal? How did they clothe themselves and create a ball complete with an orchestra and punch bowls? She knew ghosts had the ability to move objects. If they tried hard enough, they could manifest into a transparent figure of their former selves. But she'd never seen an instance where they manifested into physical beings who could touch and be touched. Who talked and interacted as if they were still alive.

Either spirits lived an entire life after death she was unaware of or something strange was going on in the mill.

She voted for strange. After seeing and talking to spirits her entire life, surely one of them would have mentioned being able to turn corporeal and touch a living human. Yep, definitely. They often mentioned how much they missed being touched.

Which brought her back to her original question. How did Luca create the party and make the guests turn into physical beings? And why would he keep it a secret?

Well, that part was easy. He might find her as attractive as she found him, but he did not yet know her well enough to explain his illusionary skill. Her mission tonight—provided he asked her to another party—was to convince him to open up to her, to tell her his secrets.

Sharing is a give-and-take proposition, a little voice in her head intoned.

Crap. How could she expect Luca to share his entire story when she refused to mention why she'd fled to Italy? In order to discover his secret, she needed to tell him hers, needed to admit her failure. The thought sent a cascade of chills through her body, as if she fell through ice into a frozen lake.

****

Luca leaned against the outside wall of the winery, legs stretched out, and stared across the vineyard. Years ago, he'd tended land like this on a plot nearby before working for the Romanis. Life had been pleasant back then. Tend the fields. Bring in the crops. Work in the mill office keeping books.

A good life filled with purpose.

Unlike now. Now he floated around the grounds, longing to see the graves of his family, wishing he could feel the brush of wheat against his skin, the rough dirt against his fingers. His main purpose was to keep from going crazy trapped upon this land.

Some days he failed. More often than not lately.

Then Adrianna had appeared and brought hope to his endless existence. Dancing with her last night had been the highlight of his life. Not even his long dead fiancée had compared to how he felt with Adrianna. He'd wanted the party to last forever, to hold her in his arms, the touch of her body a balm against his soul.

The hard stones pressed against his back, an uncomfortable reminder of where he sat. The resting place allowed a good distance between him and Adrianna. The longer he stood in her presence, the more he liked her, the more he wanted to spend the rest of his life holding her close. A man's desire, not a ghost's. A ghost should know better than to crave the living. But the man in him wanted the comfort of a woman.

Of Adrianna.

His attraction to her distracted him from his mission to obtain his freedom. Not admitting his true purpose in wanting to meet her would lead to problems if he continued to let his attraction grow. But if he told her she was the key to his freedom and she rejected him, then what would he do? How could he continue in his half life without abandoning his moral code and becoming like Marco? His brother had given up, given in to the seductive voice of evil. He held on to hope. Adrianna had said she had cousins, but they never visited the property. He needed to perform a selfless act for a person of Romani blood to ensure his freedom.

But how? Designing an illusionary trap to save her from would not fall under the category of a selfless act. What if she left before freeing him? What if she didn't care to free him?

No, last night he'd seen attraction in her gaze. She would care. But caring and action remained separate; she could care a lot and not be able to help.

He closed his eyes and rubbed the bridge of his nose.

"You've been melancholy of late, brother."

Why did Marco always appear when least wanted? He silently cursed at his brother's intrusion. Marco loomed next to him, staring down with hands on his hips, a cocky smirk on his face.

"You've been following me around of late."

Marco raised a brow. "And this makes you melancholy?"

"No. It makes me want to be left alone."

"Testy, I see. You clearly did not have a woman last night."

Ah, but he had. In a way. Just not the way his brother meant. He shrugged. "You mean a spirit?"

"You jest. You know I turn the spirits into women you can touch. Perhaps you need another party to throw you out of this funk."

Ah. If there was another party, he could invite Adrianna. Except Marco would be there and see his attraction or discover the ring. He wasn't sure which was worse. He'd never hear the end of it if his brother learned how much he enjoyed Adrianna's company. And he feared for her if Marco saw Dario's ring on her finger.

Ignoring his brother's question, he countered with one of his own. "Did you enjoy yourself last night? Others said you left with Lydia."

Marco grinned as he lowered himself to the ground. "Ah, yes. My evening was enjoyable. I would not be opposed to seeing her again."

"If you held another party and she came, would you enjoy yourself again? Or do you tire of her company?"

"I have not yet tired of her." Marco's smile widened as a devious gleam sparked his eyes. "I will create another party tonight and invite Lydia. You will find yourself a woman and throw away this melancholy. Yes?"

He stared at his brother as a grin curved his lips. Once Marco left with Lydia, he would ask Adrianna to attend. Dancing with her and seeing what she knew about the ring and Dario's curse became tonight's goals. With a little luck he would obtain the information he needed and not alienate her to his attentions. After so long without a focus, it felt good to have a purpose other than keeping himself from going crazy. He nodded.

"Yes. I will attend. And dance."

"Good." Marco barked a laugh, slapping his hands

against his thighs. "I will drink well tonight. Parties give me such a rush of energy. One day soon I will be able to break the curse on my own. And then the Romani descendants will rue the day Dario cursed us. Until tonight, brother."

He slapped Luca's thigh before disappearing.

The cold fist clutching his stomach tightened its grip. Now he had another purpose—stop Marco from gaining power.

No problem. If only he knew how Marco accumulated that power in the first place.

Chapter Six

Once the sun set and darkness crept across the grounds, Adrianna opened the shutters of the window behind the table. She turned a chair to face the window and plopped into the cushioned seat. Ready and waiting for Luca to appear and ask her to dance. She'd spent the afternoon and evening working up the courage to share her secret with him if necessary. Hopefully it wouldn't be necessary. Maybe he would spill his guts, leaving hers in place.

And the chances of that happening vacillated between slim and none. She reached deep inside, wrapping herself in a thin layer of courage.

Light from the lamps on the nightstands cast a glow across the wall, elongating her shadow. According to her phone, she sat in the chair for over an hour reading her book and waiting. Right when she was going to give up and go to bed, lights began flickering in the abandoned wing of the mill. The swell of stringed instruments playing a waltz drifted from out of the tunnel. Her eyes strained against the dim light. Where was Luca? Would he appear, or was her wait for nothing?

A shadow across the courtyard oscillated to the beat of the music. She squinted. Was it him? A trick of the light? Wind rustling tree limbs? The shadow stopped moving, expanding outward as it ran up the wall, disappearing into the vines drooping from the ruined roof.

She jerked back in her chair. Her breath caught in her throat. One hand reached for the paneled shutters in a futile attempt to block whatever ran up the wall from seeing her. She started to rise when Luca appeared where only seconds before the shadow stood.

Breath whooshed out of her lungs. He came. Furthermore, he wasn't the creepy-ass shadow.

She waved to him, gave him the "just a minute" gesture before closing the shutters. Leaving the light on, she hurried out the door, locking it behind her. Warm, humid air brushed against her skin like a soft, snug shirt. She slipped the key into the pocket of her capris and darted to where Luca stood, her shoes *flip-flop-flipping*, an accompaniment to the chirping insects and drifting strands of music.

"Hello." The low tone of his voice wrapped around her with strands of promise.

A shiver of desire weaved through her veins, heating her core. She halted a couple of feet from him, arms moving as if to wrap him in a hug. His transparent state proved the idiocy of that idea. Later. Definitely later.

She shuffled her feet, dropping her arms. "Hello to you too. I take it there's another party?"

He grinned. "There is. Do you wish to attend?"

"I'd love to. Will you create me a ball gown?"

"Of course. Come. Let's dance the night away."

Like the previous evening, he led her under the arch and down the stairs. Lights glimmered from the tunnel entrance, welcoming them to the party. The scent of damp stones gave way to cake-scented air. Clearly a trick like the not-really-there punch bowl. A trick she'd missed last night when all the sights and sounds overwhelmed her senses.

The tunnel continued to emit its creepy "stay away" spell. She ignored the pinpricks of warning dancing across her skin, prickling her flesh into thousands of goosebumps, as she passed into the tunnel. Too many spirits in one place at one time caused a tingling sensation, like an electrical short along her nerves. Although this sensation was different, darker, more potent.

She shoved the thought to the side, into the "deal with it tomorrow" part of her mind. Tonight, she held the hand of the hottest ghost in the place. First up on her to-do list was asking said ghostly hunk how he created the illusion of a ball complete with physical bodies for unsolid beings.

When they stepped out of the tunnel and into the ballroom, she wore a rose-colored gown, the hem brushing against her ankles. Ballet-like slippers graced her feet. Luca wore the same tux as the night before or a similar one. Totally hot. She could get used to the magic turning his body solid. A little too used to it.

She gave herself a mental headshake. Nope. Not going there. For tonight she was living in the moment. Enjoying being with a man who she could easily fall for if he lived.

Yet another problem to deal with tomorrow. Tomorrow's "deal with it" list grew longer every moment.

Enough of hiding behind her thoughts. Focusing on the hot man beside her was more fun. She turned to Luca. "What did you do during the day?"

"Nothing much. Toured the vineyard and winery."

Her eyes widened. "During the day? You were outside during the day?"

No ghost she knew could leave the confines of their house during the day. Sunlight trapped them inside like a physical barrier.

His lips tightened as he grabbed her hand, whirling her onto the crowded dance floor. "I'm not like most ghosts."

"How so?" Interesting. And yet not surprising. He possessed abilities Adrianna had never seen in other spirits. Or living humans for that matter.

Luca glanced over her shoulder as he twirled her in a tight circle, his silence speaking volumes. Unlike last night, she wouldn't give up until she got answers.

His gaze met and held hers as his jaw tightened. His low-pitched words shot adrenaline through her veins. "I'm a cursed man, not a dead one."

She stopped. He stumbled a step before pulling her off the dance floor. Dancers whirled past, gowns flaring as they spun, none noticing the shock stunning her motionless. She forced her gaping mouth closed. Surely she'd misheard. Had he said he was cursed? Implied he had not died? How could someone be cursed for a century and appear non-corporeal?

"I see my situation bothers you."

She swallowed. "No, not bothers. Surprises me. I've never met a cursed person." At least not one cursed like him. "How did it happen?"

He sighed. "Would you care to sit? It is a long story."

She nodded, letting him lead her to a sofa set against the wall. She hadn't realized her determination to discover how he created such strong illusions would lead to this answer. Cursed? Dead with problems, she could deal with; dead and pissed off, no problem. But cursed into a spirit without dying first? How did that even happen?

He dropped her hand and took the spot next to her on the loveseat, his knees touching the satiny folds of her gown. A muscle ticked in his jaw. She rested her hand on his knee, the touch an attempt at comfort and support. His eyes widened for a moment as he looked at her hand, then he laced his fingers through hers, releasing a long sigh.

"You might see me differently at the end of my story."

"Did you kill someone in cold blood?"

"No!" His brows pulled together. "Why would you jump to that assumption?"

She squeezed his hand. "If your story involves you killing someone in cold blood, then yes, I will see you differently. If it doesn't, then I won't. Either way, I'd like to hear what happened."

His expression relaxed as he gazed across the room to where a group of ghosts clustered around the punch bowl, talking but not drinking. After a moment he met her eyes. "My brother, Marco, and I worked in the mill for years. I was the bookkeeper, and he the manager. But in 1910, Marco…um, displeased…the owner. Who cursed us. And here we are."

She blinked. "Say what?" She cleared her throat. "I'm sorry. Did you say the mill's owner cursed you?"

He nodded. "He cursed Marco. I was standing beside him, and the same curse hit me."

Okay. How the hell was he cursed into a ghost-like

state? She shifted on the cushioned seat and cleared her throat again. The existence of a cursed human happened, more than she wanted to admit. But a human who was cursed to be a ghost?

"You're not a ghost. Not really."

"For all intents and purposes, I am." His shoulders slumped. "The living cannot see me. I cannot talk to them. I cannot touch them."

"You're touching me." She raised their laced fingers. "How can you do this if you can't touch the living?"

Another glance to the punch bowl. "I am not sure. Truth be told, I am surprised it worked on you."

"You don't know how you created this ball?" Her hand swept in a half circle to include the room and all the spirits.

"I did not create it." He shook his head, gaze hardening. "Marco creates it. I created your gown and my suit. I wanted to talk with you last night but wasn't certain you could pass through the tunnel entrance and turn into one of us."

"Wait a minute. You didn't know what would happen to me if I walked into the tunnel?"

"No, no. I did not know if you could pass through the entrance. Most living humans cannot. Some of the workers have tried but are unable to walk farther than a couple of feet into the tunnel. There's a spell in place to keep out prying eyes. Nothing would have happened to you, except you could not have attended the party. I would never hurt you."

She believed him. Maybe she shouldn't. Maybe she should run screaming from the room. But her belief stemmed from the truth shining in his eyes, from the way she felt safe in his presence.

Unless she saw what she wanted to believe. Unless she misjudged him like she misjudged her client's boyfriend, leading to the client's death and her subsequent flight to Italy.

The difference being she'd never met the boyfriend.

"Is the tunnel entrance some sort of a portal?" Skipping right over whether or not he spoke the truth and whether or not she believed him, she struck at the root of what mattered.

"A gate between worlds, in a manner of speaking. It allows spirits to become corporeal as they pass into the room. They enjoy coming here since it allows them the pleasure of touching and being touched. Marco and I are always able to touch each other, but the others cannot outside of these parties."

Adrianna stared around the room, trying to see past the illusion, trying to understand what powered it. "You really don't know how your brother creates all this?"

He shook his head. "I have my suspicions. I am able to create small things, like the illusion of paintings or books, but nothing on this grand of a scale. Marco will not tell me how he does it." He gestured toward the dancers.

She slowly nodded as she continued to look around the room. So much for learning how this place was created. Sure, in theory she could find and ask Marco. But the way Luca spoke of his brother, the hard glint in his eyes when he mentioned his name, made her not want to meet the man, ghost, whatever.

A connection fired in her brain. Her eyes widened at the implication. "Were you and Marco in my room when I first arrived? Was he the one who knocked over the lamp?"

Luca's lips pressed tight. His grip tightened against her fingers before releasing. "He thought it funny to scare you. I chased him out of the room."

A sensation of melting ice slithered down her spine. Evil. His brother was the demonic entity.

"I am sorry." He turned to face her. "He scares you."

Not the frightened, heart-thudding, breath-frozen experience typical of being scared, more like being cautious when driving through a bad part of town in the middle of the night.

"He's evil. Was that why he was cursed?"

He closed his eyes, a muscle twitching his jaw. "He tried to kill the mill's owner. Marco thought he could become the owner with Dario Romani gone."

"He tried to kill my great-grandfather?" And in retaliation Dario cursed them. Was this part of the stories about the mill Maria and Luigi had mentioned?

"Dario was your great-grandfather?"

"Yes." She nodded. "Answer the question. Please."

"He tried. According to Dario. Marco still denies it." Tension rippled through his jaw.

"And you? What do you believe?"

He ran his free hand over his head and stared at the ceiling. After a long pause, he drew in a breath and faced her. "At first I believed Marco. He was my older brother whom I looked up to. Why wouldn't I believe him? But Dario's words sank deep. The man was infuriated. He hurled his curse at Marco without seeming to care I stood beside him. Years later, I realized he was so mad he did not see me until it was too late." He brushed a strand of hair from her face. "What do you think of this tale of two brothers cursed to a half life, neither living nor dead?"

"I think it sad. You were in the wrong place at the wrong time." Her brows gathered in a tight vee. "What happened to your bodies?"

He appeared taken aback by the question but only for a brief moment. "I do not know. When I woke lying on the floor of the mill office, I no longer had the ability to touch anything. My hand went right through everything. Marco was in the same state. When cursed into a life as a spirit, you forget to look for your body until it's too late."

"Where's Marco now?" She didn't feel a demonic presence, but if he appeared at the ball, she wanted to escape to her warded room.

A half smile tugged the corners of Luca's lips. "He has a ghost lover. He is occupied for the evening."

She nodded, relief creeping across her limbs. Once she returned to the apartment, she would strengthen the wards around the place. Keep the evil, cursed creature away from her until she discovered a banishing spell.

A banishing spell was not difficult to cast, unlike finding a spell to free Luca. During her tenure as a medium, she'd cast a few banishing spells, trapping the evil spirits who roamed the streets of New York City and sending them to Hell. During all that time, never once had she freed a cursed spirit.

Hell, she'd never met a cursed spirit like Luca. How did one free a human cursed into a ghost-like existence?

Whatever the way, she'd find it. He deserved freedom, deserved to live life as a human, not a non-corporeal being longing for the touch of the living.

Tomorrow, she would work on solving his problem. Tonight, she planned to enjoy the rest of the evening.

She placed her other hand on top of their entwined fingers. "Want to dance?"

Chapter Seven

Luca led Adrianna back to the dance floor, an ache setting up residence behind his ribs, as if his heart pounded from exertion. Which shouldn't happen to a ghost but had occurred on a regular basis to him over the last century. Another oddity in his life.

He pulled her closer than what was considered polite in his day, enjoying the feel of her body pressed against his. Her pulse raced through the large vein in her neck as a flush spread across her cheeks. Her gaze met his, unafraid of him even after hearing his tale. Yet despite her nonchalant words, he had seen fear in her expression when she realized Marco had knocked over the lamp in her room. Instead of running away, abandoning the place to his fury, she clearly shoved her fear aside. He admired her courage in the face of his brother's wrath.

Marco might be his brother, but if he believed Luca crossed him, their relationship would not save him.

"How often do you throw these parties?" Her brown eyes focused with the intent of a spider on its prey.

Why all the questions about the party? "Whenever Marco decides to throw them. He found me melancholy and decided a party would cheer me up."

Her eyes widened. "Are you sad?"

"Not at the moment." He grinned.

She shook her head. "I'd hope not." Her gaze flickered over his shoulder for a second. "It must be difficult for you."

"It is. I remember what it was like. How it felt to be alive." Was he sharing too much too soon? Her attention focused on him, though, so perhaps his worry was for naught.

"In all your years here, have any of the spirits mentioned a way to free you from the curse?"

He shook his head. "They do not know." He spoke the truth. No spirit had ever mentioned a way to break the spell. Why would they? Only Dario had given him an exit plan. And he was not ready to share that information. Until he knew for certain she was willing to help him, he would keep silent. Besides, he still needed to figure out what kind of selfless act to perform.

Her lips tightened, her gaze growing distant. "There has to be a way. Someone must know something." She straightened. "Maybe Dario wrote down the spell. I will ask Maria and Luigi if they found his belongings."

"You will help me?" A glimmer of hope caught in his chest, a hope he thought destroyed over the years.

"Of course. You don't belong here with the others. They aren't like you."

He looked around the room, at the spirits swaying to the music on the crowded dance floor, to the musicians playing instruments as well in death as they had in life. How right she was. "No. They are not like me."

Her mouth opened as if to speak, but the chiming of the clock halted her words. The music stopped, and everyone else walked to the tunnel to stand in a line to exit. Was the evening over already? Too soon. Spending time with her, sharing his life, made the clock appear to run faster.

"We must leave." He kept his arm around her waist, pulling her closer, not wanting the sensation of her skin against his to stop. Even though he knew they needed to leave.

Now.

Marco always returned at the end of the evening. Always checked on the large room to ensure no one remained. He did not need to know Adrianna had attended. He needed to believe she remained in her apartment oblivious to the gathering of the ghosts. Luca doubted any of the attending spirits would tell his brother a living woman came to their party, so unless Marco saw her himself, he would believe she stayed in the apartment.

She hesitated. Luca tugged her forward until they stood in the exit line.

"What's the rush?"

Lowering his head, he whispered in her ear, "Marco returns."

She straightened, sucking in a noisy breath. "Okay."

Luca hated scaring her, using the threat of his brother, but she must be back in her room before he returned.

Once again, she hesitated. What was wrong? He glanced over his shoulder. No Marco. Praise God and the Saints. No other spirits either.

"What—?"

The words died on his lips as she wrapped a hand

around the nape of his neck, stood on her tiptoes, and pressed her lips against his. Warmth spread outward from where their lips touched. Startled, but only for a moment, he wrapped his arms around her waist and pulled her close. Desire pulsed through his veins, centering in his cock. He wanted her. Now.

And how's that going to work for you, Luca?

Damn little mind voice. Ruining his perfect moment. Although it spoke the truth. Once they passed through the tunnel, he would revert to his transparent state. And there wasn't a chance in hell he would take her on the wooden floor of the ballroom.

Not to mention, the end of the illusion heralded the arrival of his brother.

What he needed was a way to get her to his room in the back of the cavern without Marco noticing.

If wishes came true, he'd be free.

Using his remaining willpower, he ended the kiss. His heart pounded an erratic rhythm.

"I could kiss you all night, but we need to go. Now."

Her eyes grew large as she glanced around the empty ballroom. "You're right. Let's go."

They hurried through the tunnel, his form losing its corporeality when they exited. Once again a ghost. Madonna help him.

His suit faded to his regular outfit of shirt and trousers, the clothing he'd been wearing when cursed. Likewise, Adrianna's gown disappeared into her T-shirt and calf-length pants.

Together they darted up the stairs and across the grass to her door. She reached into her pocket and pulled out the key.

"Will I see you again tomorrow?" Dark brown eyes held his attention.

"If you'd like." *Please say you'd like.*

Her brows arched. "I'd definitely like to see you again. Do you want to see me?"

Yes! Instead of jumping up and down like a child presented with a piece of candy, he nodded. "Very much so. Until tomorrow, then."

She gave him a small smile. "Sleep well."

"I do not—"

"I know. Sorry. It was a joke."

A shift in the air told him Marco neared. "Hurry. Go inside. Now. Go."

A moment later, she shut and locked the door. He flew across the dew-dampened grass to the other side of the pool. Flying was one of the few things he liked about being a cursed spirit. The speed allowed him to move much faster than walking or running. Wind blew his hair off his forehead, whispered like the soft touch of a woman against his skin.

He might like the ease of movement but not enough to want to remain a ghost.

He lowered himself onto a deck chair, watching as the sun rose over the horizon. A shimmering brown-orange light oscillated over the ruined wing of the mill, right above where the party had occurred. Marco. Visiting the large underground cavern to ensure no one remained.

Earlier, he'd fudged the answer to Adrianna's question about how Marco created the illusion. While his brother never told him how he turned spirits into physical beings or weaved a delightful illusion of a late nineteenth century ball, he suspected the answer.

Somehow Marco managed to steal the ghosts' energies, to gather enough power to fuel the party with plenty left over.

He used the same theory to create Adrianna's gown, but unlike his brother, he drew his creation energy from the surrounding nature. Sitting in the vineyard, watching the grapes grow, replenished what he'd lost. Nature allowed him to turn his little underground room off the main cavern area into an art museum. An illusion he could only maintain while in the room and only for a few hours. Marco maintained parties for hours at a time whether or not he was in attendance and, in his words, drank deeply from the night's activities.

Evil. Somewhere in the long years of his life, his brother had turned evil. Demonic. Like one of those vampires he saw featured on popular television shows.

The lights above the mill stopped shimmering as dawn cast an orange-pink light across the horizon. A shadow expanded outward, darkening the grass as it sped toward him. Tingles spread across his skin as Marco approached.

He straightened, sitting upright on the edge of the lounger. Illusions meant the world to Marco. Including his own deception. "Brother. How was your evening?"

Marco materialized next to him, slapping a hand against his shoulder. "Pleasant enough. And yours? You no longer look melancholy."

He swallowed and forced a grin. "You were right. An evening spent dancing with a lovely woman was what I needed."

Marco sat on the adjoining lounger, leaning his elbows against his knees. "See? I told you." A grin turned his lips into a parody of a smile. "I am almost ready, brother. Soon I will be able to break this curse, to turn it against the one who cast it."

Not this again. Why couldn't Marco try to change his present circumstances instead of seek revenge? He suppressed a headshake. "Dario is long dead."

"The sins of the forefathers must be passed down to their offspring."

"What are you planning?" He gripped the edge of the lounger, crushing the cushion under his fingers.

Marco shrugged. "Death. They can join us in this afterlife."

Why was he so fixated on Dario's descendants? Why not use his energy to escape the curse? "I thought you said you would free us."

"Their deaths will free us. Free us to heap anguish upon them. Forever. They will be trapped here forever. With us." He laughed, the noise running like fingernails across the chalkboard of Luca's spine.

He released his grip on the cushion before Marco noticed his anger and shook his head. "I don't want to trap them. I want to be free."

"You never could see the bigger picture." Marco glared at him. "If Dario had not grown wise to my plot, we would have owned this place. All of it. The vineyards. The manor house. The farmlands. Everything. Ours."

He closed his gaping mouth. Finally. Marco admitted what Dario had said all those years ago. What he'd known as truth for decades. But playing the part of the adoring younger brother meant he needed to act surprised Dario told the truth instead of shocked about what Marco admitted.

At least the shock wasn't feigned. "So all this time, Dario spoke the truth?"

"Luca, Luca, Luca." Marco shook his head. "You believe what you want to believe. You don't look for the truth. Of course, I tried to kill him. He was a worthless landowner. I would have been better. Made more money by charging higher land rents. Don't look so surprised. We will get our revenge. Not much longer now. You'll see. Then you will no longer be melancholy."

Marco gave him a pat on the leg. As if he were still the innocent younger brother. Had Marco ever seen him as equal? Or had he always been the dupe in his brother's plans?

A muscle in his jaw ticked a throbbing rhythm as he stared at the creature sitting across from him. Marco looked human, albeit a transparent one, but his soul belonged to the devil himself.

He refused to let Marco harm Adrianna. Refused to allow him to reverse engineer a curse. But how did he stop Marco's plan?

He glared at his brother until the demonic creature vanished, leaving behind a lingering chill of laughter.

Chapter Eight

Adrianna woke to alarm music on her phone. She rolled over and swiped the off button. Placing both hands over her face, she rubbed her head until the dream vanished from her sleep-induced haze. Two in the afternoon seemed early.

But at least she'd be awake and showered before Maria stopped by.

Before going to sleep last night—oops, this morning—she'd sent Maria a text asking if they had any of Dario's belongings, and if so, would Maria bring them when she dropped off dinner? A quick check of her phone showed no response.

Dammit. Had Maria not received the message or received it and decided not to respond?

Crushing the urge to send another text—after all, Maria would be here in an hour or so—she climbed out of bed and headed for the shower. Once finished, she went to work strengthening the wards around her room. She'd rushed the words this morning after Luca walked her to the door, his sense of urgency bleeding into her veins as she spoke the words of the spell. Rushing a spell, especially when sleepy, meant she might have made a mistake in her haste to complete it before Marco arrived.

Luckily, he'd left her alone. But who knew how long the reprieve would last?

Best to finish prior to Maria arriving. While the Toscanos supported her psychic abilities, she had no doubt they'd freak over her speaking spells of protection. Unless those spells came with a benediction to the saints.

She shook her head as she walked around the room, performing the spell to keep evil away from her apartment. When she finished, she grabbed a towel, walked outside to the pool, and flopped in one of the loungers.

Unlike yesterday when she swam laps, she used the relaxing atmosphere of the pool to center her thoughts. To plot a way to help free Luca from the curse.

How odd her great-grandfather—a man she'd never met but heard multiple stories about—had spoken a curse turning two men into phantoms. She thought herself the only one in her family with psychic abilities. Her grandfather hadn't possessed the ability to see ghosts, and as far as she knew, neither had her parents. At least her grandfather had never said anything about it. Then again, he'd never told her about any of the mill stories the Toscanos mentioned.

Clearly Dario was the reason she was able to see otherworldly beings. The average person could never turn humans into phantoms without killing them. That type of curse required a huge amount of power only a psychic could conjure.

A damn powerful psychic. She thought of herself as a badass medium, but she couldn't cast a spell like Dario's curse.

How the hell was she going to help Luca if she couldn't recreate the original spell?

She ran a hand through her tight curls. Well, she'd

come to Italy to escape New York and get away from ghosts, and look what happened.

Now she was determined to help one.

Water rippled across the pool from the breeze. Leaves rustled as birds hopped from limb to limb. The relaxing sights and sounds eased her swirling thoughts. A little bit of calm helped her think. The gentle brush of a breeze against her skin made her want to close her eyes. Why not? Stressing over Luca's problem would not help her find a solution. She leaned back against the cushions, closing her eyes. After having slept most of the day, she should be awake and ready to run. Instead, tension drained from her limbs as she listened to the sounds of nature and the gentle lapping of water against the edges of the pool.

A high-pitched humming interrupted her peace. Was that a car? As the noise gathered in pitch and intensity, she opened her eyes. Nope. Not a car. The humming now sounded like a million insects buzzed a cacophony. Except she couldn't see any bugs. Not even a fly or a spider crawled across the tiled deck. She sat upright, turning to look at the trees behind her. Leaves rustled, moving as if a strong wind blew, even though the breeze remained gentle against her skin. Twittering birds no longer hopped from limb to limb. No birds. No bugs. Only the weird buzzing noise.

Shit.

She jumped up, meaning to run to the safety of her apartment, when the water in the pool rose into a huge towering wave. Drawing in a deep breath, she centered herself. No way could she make it to her apartment before the evil spirit attacked. Fighting was her only option. Ice flowed through her veins as she straightened and pulled in energy from the surrounding nature. She knew how to fight Marco, knew the spells to use to break his concentration, to make him stop his attempt at a frightening display.

Attempt at a frightening display? Who was she kidding? She was a skilled medium, and this display pretty much scared the shit right out of her.

Shoving her hand out before her in a stop-right-there motion, she drew more energy from the land, funneling it outward through her palm. "Stop!"

The tower of water grew.

She funneled even more energy into her palm, her body vibrating with power, and pushed it toward Marco. "I. Said. Stop!"

The buzzing noise reached a crescendo. Air pulsed a throbbing beat against her skin. Tingles ran up her arm as the creature's power searched for a way under her flesh. She shoved energy harder at the pissed-off spirit.

"Leave!" A deep voice roared out of the water as the wave crashed into her, knocking her back a step.

She sputtered, swiping the water off her face, her concentration shattered. A cold blanket of terror twisted around her as the spirit swirled in a tight circle, closer and closer. Her heart pounded an erratic beat as she stifled a scream. He wanted her to scream, and she'd be damned if she gave him the pleasure.

"I said, leave!" This time the voice whispered the command in her ear, following it up with a shove.

But she was ready. No freaking ghost was going to scare her away from her family's property. From the coolest place she'd ever lived. Nope, not happening. She grabbed another round of energy from the earth and using her body as a conduit of power, slammed that energy into the spirit.

Instead of her flying backward from his shove, he flew backward with a sharp pop, the discharge turning him visible for a moment as he landed in the grass on the other side of the pool. Black eyes glared at her as he propped himself on one elbow. Pain etched lines in his face. A snarl rippled across his lip. From one blink of her eyes to the next, he vanished.

She released a pent-up breath of air. Adrenaline continued to race through her veins even as her knees wobbled. She butt-planted on the lounger and sucked in several deep breaths. She'd won. Chasing off the evil entity was well worth the resulting ball of writhing snakes slithering in her stomach.

Her eyes widened as her spine stiffened, and she leapt from the chair. What if he returned? What if she'd put a temporary hurt on him but he came zipping back even stronger than before?

Breath caught in her lungs. Drained of energy, would she be able to drive him away if he returned? Probably not.

She grabbed the towel off the chair and dashed across the grass to her apartment. She darted inside, slamming the door behind her, and leaned against it, her heart pounding a marathon. *Safe.*

She hoped.

Her wards would hold. She'd cast plenty of warding spells before for clients, albeit with more candles and incense, and her spells always held. It would hold this time too.

Be confident in your skills, Adrianna.

At one time she had been. Before her fatal mistake.

Well, what she had done once before, she could do again.

A *drip-drip-drip* against tile snapped her attention to the small puddle of water under her feet. Right. Marco had thrown half the pool water at her. Time to change into something dry. Dry clothes meant more confidence, and she needed a boost at the moment.

She pulled a change of clothes from the dresser and walked into the bathroom. After changing, she hung the still dripping bathing suit over the edge of the tub and opened the door. Only to suck in a gasp of air.

Luca sat on the bed. His gaze ran over her body in a clinical way as he stood. "I wanted to make sure you were all right."

"You startled me." Taking a step into the room, she pulled the bathroom door shut.

"My apologies. Are you all right?"

"Just a little startled. It's okay." Unless he meant her fight at the pool? "Wait. Do you know what happened just a minute ago?"

His eyes narrowed as his nostrils flared. "Not when it happened. But I know you hurt Marco. How did you do it?"

"Are you upset I hurt him?" While Marco deserved what he'd gotten plus some, she didn't want Luca upset with her.

Gah. She'd definitely fallen hard for the ghost if she was asking that question.

"No."

Tension fled her limbs at his answer. Double *gah.*

He continued, apparently unaware of her silent conflict. "Marco told me he tried to scare you. He deserved whatever you did to him. He wants you gone."

She passed him to sit in one of the comfy chairs by the fireplace. "I got that impression. A giant tower of water telling you to leave tends to clue you in."

She started to turn to face him when he appeared in the chair next to hers. A gasp escaped her lips. "Give me some warning next time."

He grinned. "As you wish." His grin faded as his expression turned serious. "I am sorry I was not there to protect you. Although you seemed to do a good enough job protecting yourself. How did you hurt him?"

"How bad did I hurt him?" Was it permanent? Or equivalent to a punch to the face? Painful, but quick to recover?

He shrugged. "He'll be fine by tomorrow evening."

She nodded. *Dammit*. She really wanted the permanent option as an answer. Hurting people wasn't in her playbook, but Marco wasn't a person. Or even a normal, but moody, everyday spirit. He was evil. And evil needed to be sent back to where it came from in whatever way possible.

"To answer your question, I gathered energy and shoved it into him right when he shoved energy to me. He was trying to push me over. When my energy met his, there was this *pop*, and he flew backward. He actually became visible for a moment." Her flesh crawled at the memory.

He glanced at her hands. A fine wrinkle formed between his brows. "Did you shove him with one hand or two?"

She waved her right hand. "This one." The red stone on her grandfather's family ring shimmered in the light.

His expression shuttered, hiding his thoughts. Was

91

there some connection between him and her family ring? She glanced at the ring. Nothing looked different about it. Same red stone. Same family crest etched in the gold. Same weight and feel on her finger. Maybe he recognized the ring from when her great-grandfather wore it, and it brought back memories.

She met his hazel eyes. "Why?"

"Perhaps the ring contains a power of its own." His no-big-deal shrug sent prickles of awareness across her consciousness.

She glanced at her right hand again. Besides the age and monetary value, what was special about the old ring? She looked at him. "What do you know?"

Bam, bam, bam! "Adrianna! Are you awake?"

They both jumped at the knock and Maria's call.

Shit. Could the woman's timing be any worse?

"Just a second!" she yelled. "Can she see you?" she whispered.

He shrugged and shook his head.

Okay, then. While Maria definitely felt the brothers' fight the other evening—even the most unbelieving person would've noticed—she didn't seem to see them, so hopefully she wouldn't notice him sitting in the chair.

She held a finger over her lips, and he nodded. She hurried to the door and glanced at him, one hand on the knob. He winked and faded out of sight, a slight glow hovering above the chair indicating he remained in the room. Well, that solved the problem of whether or not Maria could see him. She barely noticed him sitting in the chair. Plastering a smile on her face, she opened the door, and stepped back to allow Maria inside.

The older woman carried a large container, a

pleasing aroma of tomato sauce and cheese escaping the foil cover. If she didn't stop eating Maria's delicious meals, she was going to gain a hundred pounds.

"It smells wonderful. What did you make?" Adrianna closed the door as Maria set the container on the counter.

"*Penne all'arrabbiata.*"

"Yum." She loved the spicy tomato sauce. "Are you staying for dinner?"

"No. Not tonight." Maria huffed, the corners of her lips pulling down. "Something broke at the winery, and we have to fix it."

"Oh no! Can I help?" As one of the owners, she felt she needed to assist with problems. Not that she had a clue how to help—her only handyman skills involved hammering nails into walls to hang paintings—but she needed to do something.

Maria raised a brow. "It's not your concern."

Come again? Surely it was her concern. She crossed her arms. "I'm part owner of the winery. I need to become more active in my role."

"No!" Maria slashed a hand through the air. "You are on vacation. Rest. You still look tired. New York did not treat you well."

She jerked as if slapped. Being told not to take an active role in running the properties was a bit disconcerting. But more important, did Maria know about the event causing her to flee to Italy? Or was she just concerned by her appearance and had no clue about her recent troubles?

After a couple of eye blinks and deep breaths, she voted for the latter.

"All right." She drew out the words. "But at some

point, I need to tour the properties. Grandfather would want me to."

"Yes, yes. Just not now." Maria headed toward the door.

A thought jolted her. She almost forgot to ask. Having a tower of water thrown at her by an irate spirit and being told to ignore her duties tended to make a person distracted.

"Did you get my text this morning?"

Maria paused, one hand on the doorknob as she stared where Luca sat. "Yes, yes. Sorry." She squinted at the chair for longer than Adrianna liked.

Could Maria actually see Luca? Adrianna followed her gaze. Luca sat as a shadow lined with a blue-green glow. Not something a non-psychic person would notice. And yet Maria continued to stare at him as if he sat in full view.

After a long moment, her attention returned to Adrianna. "We don't have anything of Dario's. All his things were divided among his children. What exactly were you wanting?"

Any information related to his ability to write and cast curses. Did he write a grimoire? You know, the normal things a relative wanted to see. Yeah, right. Like she was going to say anything remotely close to the truth.

"He owned this place, right? I wanted to see if there were any records or bookkeeping. You know, stuff like that."

Raising a brow, Maria stared at her. "You want to read business ledgers? *Pfft.*" She waved a hand. "Boring. Unless you are an attorney. Which you aren't. Go sit by the pool. Relax. Enjoy the beautiful weather."

She gave Adrianna a hug. "Stop worrying. Relax. Enjoy." Her gaze drifted to the chair for a second. When she met Adrianna's eyes, Maria's lips turned into a conspiratorial grin. "Enjoy, love. I'll be back tomorrow."

She stood in the doorway, watching until Maria drove down the driveway and disappeared in the distance.

Luca appeared when she closed the door.

"Maria is a good woman."

Adrianna blinked. "You know Maria?"

He shrugged. "I used to visit the manor house before they sold it. She and Luigi were there almost all the time. I have not actually met them." He gestured to his form, a bite cutting his words. "It is a little hard to meet others when I look like this."

"There's nothing wrong with how you look."

"You know that's not what I mean."

She offered him a grin as she sat beside him. "I'm just teasing you."

"I know." Luca glanced at his hands before dragging his gaze back to hers. "I overheard Luigi ask you if you were a medium. That is how you can see me, yes?"

Now it was time for her to glance at her hands. Since the appendages didn't provide an answer to the question, and she needed to woman up and share her truth, she met his gaze. "Yes. I can see you because I have psychic abilities. I can't explain how you can touch me."

One hand reached for hers, passing through her skin, leaving behind an ice-cube-like chill. His shoulders hunched forward as a sigh escaped his lips. "I

95

cannot. At least not outside of the mill during a party."

Not a surprise. The tunnel functioned as some sort of a portal during the parties, but what happened when there wasn't a party? Would he be able to touch her if they walked through the tunnel now? "If we went to the tunnel, could you touch me?"

"I do not know. Marco is there recovering." A hard grin flattened his lips.

"Okay. Definitely not now." Last thing she wanted was to run into Marco twice in a day. Once was enough. "Maybe we can test the theory after he leaves."

His gaze focused on her lips. "Maybe."

She stared at his lips, remembering his kiss, remembering the way his arms tightened around her waist, drawing her flush to his body. Remembered the shot of need ricocheting through her veins and stoking her desire. Her fingers ached to touch him again. What was it about him that drew her in as if he were an unavoidable addiction?

As a child, she'd played with ghosts—hide-and-seek in the manor house and peek-a-boo in her grandfather's home. As an adult, she'd helped them speak to loved ones or pass to the other side. They would often tell her of their lives lived, sometimes how they died, but rarely did they sit in the chair next to hers, asking her questions and carrying on a conversation like the living.

And by rarely she meant only once before with her grandfather shortly after he died. If one could call the discussion an actual conversation.

Then again, Luca said he was cursed, not dead.

Her experience with cursed spirits ranked right up there with attending a Broadway play opening night and sitting on the front row. Something others had done, but she had yet to accomplish.

Luca cleared his throat, breaking her descent into unfulfilled desire. Good thing. At least for the moment. Sitting in her apartment, staring at his lips got her nowhere fast. She needed to discover a way to break his curse and return him to the land of the living.

The grand idea to read anything Dario wrote fizzled into a dark hole of nothingness. She'd had to ask about it, though, on the off chance anything of his remained. Now that she had her answer, she needed to find another way.

Maybe one of her fellow psychic friends would know how to break a curse.

"Tell me what brought you to Italy. Maria said you needed to relax?"

Dammit. Not this again. She could fudge the answer. Claim she was returning to check out her portion of the property, and Maria mistook her visit for a need to relax. But that was mostly a lie. And she preferred truth.

Even if it meant he might see her differently.

She drew in a deep breath. She could do this. No problem. Deep breath in. Fast release out, and stare at the table instead of his eyes. *Ready, set, go.* "I'm from New York City. Lived there all my life except for summers when we'd come here. I've always been able to see the dead, and they've always talked to me. Most of them wanted closure. You know, wanted to tell their loved ones good-bye, or deliver a message, or be relieved of some burden they carried."

She twisted her grandfather's ring around her finger. "I wanted to help them. And also help the living come to grips with the death of their loved ones. It seemed only natural I would become a medium. I didn't charge much. I'd rather help others than get paid. I gained a good reputation, so my clientele list grew pretty fast."

She gave the ring another twist. The first part of her story wasn't hard to tell. But the second part, where she failed a client...She drew in another large breath. "I made a mistake. A really terrible mistake that led to the death of a client."

He reached for her hand, drawing back when it passed through her skin. Yes, his touch chilled her, but the thought behind the action lent her strength.

"What happened?" he asked at her extended pause.

Right. *Finish the story, Adrianna. Pour out your guilt.* Not that talking absolved her of the mistake.

Another deep inhale followed by an exhale of rushed words. "My client, Angela, wanted to speak to her grandmother. The grandmother, though, was one of those ghosts who spoke in riddles and was barely audible. I thought the grandmother said she loved Angela, and all was forgiven."

She waved a hand. "Spirits often deliver that same message no matter who they are or what was done. I didn't press further. But she didn't say what I thought. What she said was be careful, he's after you, and he hasn't forgiven you."

His eyes widened.

"Yeah, I know. The words don't even sound alike, but that's what I thought. During the course of the session, Angela disclosed her ex-boyfriend was stalking her. I told her to go to the police. After she left, the ex killed her and dumped her behind my office. Since I was the last person who saw her alive, the police hauled me in for questioning. The newspapers splashed my name all over the headlines.

"Speculation abounded that Angela went to see me to confirm she was safe from her boyfriend. I'm not sure who started those rumors. It's not like I told the police I misheard the grandmother. At any rate, everyone in the whole city knew who I was, and my reputation was ruined. Instead of being the go-to medium, no one came to see me at all. The notoriety got to me after a couple of weeks, and I asked Maria if I could come for a visit. She offered me this apartment, and here I am."

She met his gaze. Surprise and empathy gleamed from the hazel depths. Maybe he didn't see her differently after all.

"I'd give you a hug if I could touch you." The low tone of his voice soothed her soul.

"You're not mad?"

"Mad?" Eyes wide, he stared at her for a long moment. "No. Why would I be mad?"

She wrapped shaky arms around herself. When did she get so cold? "I thought maybe you would no longer want to see me."

He shot her a disbelieving stare. "What happened doesn't change who you are." His brows furrowed. "I would like to know how you learned what the grandmother really said."

She rubbed her hands up and down her arms. Cleared her throat. "Because she visited me every night yelling the words."

"Ah. The real reason you left New York."

For the first time in a while, she burst out laughing.

"I hope you meant that to be funny."

He shrugged, a small grin playing at the corners of his lips.

A chill continued to shiver her innards, but a lightness crept into her soul. "Thank you. For listening and not judging."

"I cannot very well judge. I have made mistakes too." His gaze hardened as he glanced to the fireplace. "I trusted Marco when I shouldn't."

"Tell me about him. About you. About growing up together."

What had he been like before the curse struck? There was so much about him she didn't know. The little details comprising the man. His likes and dislikes. Things having nothing to do with the curse.

A sad look crossed his face. Uh-oh. Maybe she shouldn't have asked about his life before the curse. Maybe he wanted to pretend that time never existed.

But he drew in a deep breath. Much like she had earlier. A need to touch him, to offer comfort through a pat on the back of his palm or a stroke along his thigh, overwhelmed her. But really, the urge would get her nowhere. She couldn't touch him. Not now.

Not until she broke the damn curse. No matter what it took, no matter how long it took, she would free him from his phantom half life.

If it was the last thing she did.

"Very well." He gestured to the no-longer-steaming food Maria had left on the counter. "You might want to grab something to eat. I can talk forever about my life."

Chapter Nine

Luca told Adrianna about growing up working the land, helping his family in the fields, bringing grain to the mill for processing. About how he and Marco, as the two eldest sons in the family, were promoted by Dario to handle the day-to-day activities of the mill. Soon, Luca was the bookkeeper and Marco the manager of the mill. Until Marco decided to kill Dario, and Dario retaliated with a curse.

Should he mention as Dario's descendant she was the key to his freedom? She was willing to help him find a way to break his curse, but he remained uncertain of her reception to knowing only she could help him. In theory, her cousins were also descendants of Dario, but never once had they visited the properties despite living a couple of hours away.

What if she thought he was using her? That he pretended to like her in order to convince her to help him? She might decide against helping him. Worse yet she might leave, never to return.

An invisible beast crushed his chest at the thought. In the few days he'd known her, she had crept into his heart, his soul, bringing light and peace to the empty darkness. What would he do without seeing her smile? To miss the way her curls framed her face? No, best to keep her role in his freedom to himself for a while longer.

"Until the curse, it sounds like you had a good life." The kind tone of her voice wrapped around him, a warm blanket of comfort.

He nodded. So many memories. So much joy.

And now, so much loneliness.

Until she brought hope.

"I did."

"What happened to your family?"

Luca closed his eyes, drew in a deep breath. Pain lanced where his heart once beat. "They died. Without knowing what happened to us. At least I assume they never knew what happened to us. I can't imagine Dario told them he cursed us into oblivion." Lips pressed together, he shook his head. "I read about their deaths in the papers, but they never knew what happened to me."

Guilt and regret swarmed around him, an infestation of biting gnats nipping at his soul. She reached out a hand, another thwarted attempt at touch he nonetheless appreciated.

"I'm sorry. I can't imagine. Did you visit their graves?"

His gaze dropped to his hands as he shook his head. "We can't leave the property. It's part of the curse."

One hand covered her mouth as her eyes widened. "Oh, Luca. I'm so, so sorry. That's even worse than them not knowing what happened to you. You weren't even able to attempt contact with them, were you?"

He shook his head. "No. I wanted to. We both wanted to. But we had to make do with following their lives via newspapers or overheard conversations. Well, I read and listened. Marco left it to me to discover what happened to our family."

Why had he not thought his brother's behavior odd at the time? Why was it only in looking back on the memories he realized evil ran through Marco even then?

"Oh, Luca." She reached for his hand again, withdrawing hers at the last second.

Another memory slapped against his skull. A dull pain, not sharp and breath-stealing. And sitting beside her, the thought no longer made his heart ache. "My fiancée married another."

"Oh, Luca. That must have really hurt." Concern shone in her brown eyes.

"It did when I first learned of it. What really hurt was how quickly she married. Not even a year passed, and she married another." He shook his head. "Now I see we were not really in love. It was more of a comfortable feeling. Once I came to that knowledge, I forgave her"—he patted his chest—"in here, since I never saw her again. Only read about her marriage and death in the papers."

"I'm so sorry."

"Enough about death." The past was the past, and talking about it got him nowhere but depressed. He'd rather talk about her. Or how society had changed over the last century.

Anything but his dead family.

"Tell me more about this electronic mail you mentioned. I have read in the papers about the internet but am not sure how it works."

Adrianna blinked. "Okay. I'm not a tech person—"

"Tech person?"

"You know…okay, I guess you don't. Technology.

A tech person is someone who knows all about technology. How computers and such work."

Ah-ha. He had seen computers before in the manor house. "Go on."

"As I was saying, I'm not a tech person, but I'll do my best to explain."

By the time dawn peeked over the horizon, he learned many new things the newspapers never explained. Not that he understood everything she said, but he understood enough to know the world had changed more than he expected. The industrial revolution had morphed into a technological one, leaving him stuck in the past.

If he managed to reverse the curse, how would he live in today's world? Societal changes, while odd, were not all unpleasant. Women wearing pants, or shorts, or the next to nonexistent swimwear, or having the right to vote and divorce seemed an inevitable advancement. All things he agreed were good improvements. Equality improved society. He could adjust to those things as well as flipping a switch to brighten a room instead of lighting a candle. But modern technology?

"I think I've overwhelmed you."

A truth if he ever heard one. "A lot has changed since I lived."

She placed a hand over her mouth as she yawned. "Someone said technology advances every eighteen months. So yes, there've been a ton of changes since 1910. You'll catch on to things. Don't worry." She yawned again.

Way to go, Luca. You've talked her to sleep. "You are tired."

A small smile curved her lips. "Yeah. You're right about that one. I'm exhausted."

"I will leave so you can sleep." Something he should have done hours ago, but damn he enjoyed talking to her, enjoyed losing himself in her world.

"You're lucky you don't have to." She stretched, pulling her arms over her head, her breasts thrusting toward him.

He swallowed. *Focus, and not on her chest.* "But I do have to rest and recharge."

"So I've heard. Will you be back tomorrow?" She stood and glanced out the window, her eyes growing round. "Oops, I mean later today?"

"If you wish."

"Oh, I wish." After a pause, she shook her head as if she wanted to say something else.

Did she wish the same thing he did? Did she want to touch him as much as he wanted to touch her? To feel the press of her lips against his, the stroke of her body as he held her tight, the pinnacle of pleasure as they joined together, was that her wish?

"Very well. I will return this evening." Perhaps Marco would be gone, and Luca could show her his room complete with the illusion of an art museum.

Maybe then he could muster the will to tell her about her part in saving him from the curse.

Maybe.

"I'm looking forward to it."

"Until then." He stood, gave her a little half bow, and walked through the wall.

Tingles shot through his body, the same as when he'd appeared earlier in her room. A spell, perhaps? Whatever the cause, the tingles pulled like a strong tug against his skin, as if encouraging him to stay away. Strange. Until she moved in, he'd never felt the little prickling jabs when he entered the apartment.

He walked into the ruined wing of the mill, passed under the arch, down the stairs, and through the tunnel. Echoes from flowing water and laughter of workers long dead drifted around the edges, a testament to the age of the building. A damp chill permeated the place and sank into his bones as he walked to the back wall. Turning left, he walked down a long hall and entered a small room. His room. The door no longer existed unless he created it, formed it out of want and will, fueled by the strength he drew from the surrounding nature. With a wave of his hand and an exhale of air, his thoughts became reality.

Paintings in gilded frames dotted the walls. A white marble sculpture of the Madonna holding a baby Christ stood in the corner. A simple wooden bed with a red and brown comforter sat against a wall. The bed reminded him of home, created years ago when such memories gave comfort. Mementoes of a past life.

He waved his hand again, and the bed disappeared. He no longer needed the memory of his bed to feel comfort and peace. Being with Adrianna tonight brought a greater pleasure than sitting on an illusionary bed, pining for the past. The past was the past. He needed to move forward, and what better way to do so than with a beautiful woman?

Provided he discovered what selfless act to perform for her benefit.

He swallowed. How hard was it to tell her what he knew? What he felt for her? Would she reject him when she learned he needed her to set him free? The desire strumming through him when in her presence twisted his gut into a knot of indecision. If he lived, he would, in the term used on the television, ask her out on a date. In his present state, the best he could hope for was another party where she could touch him.

In all the years trapped as a spirit, he'd never tried to turn into a physical being, associating the trick with Marco's unholy capability and revenge-seeking mindset. But what if he could turn into a solid being like he did at the parties?

What if he could touch her as a man, not a wispy spirit?

What if?

He glanced at the gleaming white statue.

Madonna help him.

****

Adrianna woke to chirping birds outside her window. She yawned and rolled out of bed. A quick peek at her phone showed three in the afternoon as well as a text notification. She unlocked the phone, swiped the text app, and pulled up Maria's message.

So very sorry but unable to bring dinner tonight. Are you okay on your own?

She walked to the small fridge and opened the door to an array of half-eaten dishes. Yep. Definitely okay. She could hole up in the apartment for several days with plenty to eat.

But she phrased it differently to Maria.

I'm sorry to hear I won't see you today. No problem on the food. I'll be fine. See you tomorrow?

After hitting send, she pulled up her email, checking to see if her psychic friend in New Orleans had responded to the email she sent after Luca left.

107

Yes! Her friend had responded.

She clicked on the email, leaning against the counter to read it. She sighed. Betty, or Madam Elizabeth as she liked to be called by all but close friends, was the oldest practicing medium she knew. The woman had set up practice in the 1950s when she was a teenager and still ran that practice today. They had met on a trip to New Orleans and hit it off, exchanging emails, asking each other's advice about clients. If anyone would know how to return a cursed spirit to the living, it would be Betty.

Unfortunately, Betty had no advice. While the older woman had experience with curses carrying over from a person's life into death, the cursed dead were more like Marco in personality than Luca. More demonic than good.

Unless Luca was hiding an inner Mr. Hyde.

Nah. She read people well, even cursed spirits, and Luca was not evil. A little depressed at times, but then again, who wouldn't be? If she spent the last century as a spirit confined to one property unable to visit her living relatives, unable to check on their lives, or to see them in death, she'd be a little depressed too. Hell, a little? More like a lot.

So no, he was not evil. And Betty had no idea how to help him. Which meant she was all on her own. How did one free a cursed spirit?

It would help if she knew the original curse. Oh, who was she fooling? In theory it would help. In reality she had no idea how to reverse a curse even if she knew the wording of the original spell. She rubbed the bridge of her nose.

Trying to break the curse was like following a

bramble-choked path into the woods armed with only a paring knife to slice branches. And to complicate matters, Luca attracted her like no other man had. She enjoyed their talks, getting to know him, attending the magical parties and seeing how he lived.

God help her, she had fallen for a ghost.

Talk about a relationship disaster in the making.

Nothing to it except solve the problem of freeing him. She was a smart and accomplished medium. Somehow, she would figure out a solution.

She ran a hand over her head, tugging on a curly strand of hair. Why couldn't problems come with attached solutions? Life would be so much easier.

Shaking her head, she left her phone on the counter and changed into her swimsuit. Goosebumps prickled her exposed arms and legs. Would Marco be at the pool? Part of her wanted to stay in the apartment, to avoid the chance of a visit by the furious phantom. It was a small part and easily squashed. She refused to let an evil entity control her. Refused to allow fear dominion over her ability to relax. Sitting inside the apartment, hiding behind the invisible wall of a spell, chipped away at her confidence.

She wanted to sit by the pool. Well, by God, she would walk out the door, sit by the pool, and Marco be damned.

She grabbed a towel from the bathroom and slipped on her shoes, marched out the door, up the grassy incline, and claimed her spot on a lounger. She glared at the calm water, daring Marco to appear from its depths. After a while, her brow relaxed, and she leaned back, stretching out her feet. No evil spirit. No looming tower of water. Nothing but the happy chirping of birds and gentle, barely there breeze.

Totally relaxing.

She closed her eyes, allowing her mind to roam free, to focus on Luca and the curse. But the gentle breeze and chirping birds lulled her back to sleep.

An unnatural quiet woke her. She rubbed at a throbbing sleep headache. Light shone at a different angle on the brown stones of the mill than when she'd first sat in the lounger. Had she really slept for another couple of hours? A woozy feeling, coupled with a round of nausea, swamped her. Yep, she definitely slept more than needed.

Sitting upright, she glanced around. Besides a different angle of light shining on the mill, everything looked the same as when she sat on the lounger. No pillar of water or buzzing like a thousand infuriated insects camped out in the trees. But the birds no longer sang, and an almost suffocating blanket of humidity sat heavy against her skin. Her spine solidified into a block of ice as the implication slammed into her sleep-heavy mind. Time for her to head to the apartment.

Bravery only got her so far before it crashed into stupidity.

She grabbed her towel and jogged back to the apartment as fast as possible in flip-flops. The damn shoes weren't intended to outrun a revenge-seeking demonic spirit. Halfway there, a low rumble of laughter sounded from the trees behind the pool.

Not so brave now, are you?

Nope. She was not. She picked up the pace, turning the doorknob and slamming her shoulder into the wooden panel right as a gust of cold wind carrying the stench of rotting flesh slapped her face. Nausea roiled her stomach as she stumbled into the apartment and shoved shut the door.

Bam! Wind hit the structure with a loud force, rattling the knob and hinges. The wood shook with each gust, each an attempt to break into her sanctuary. But the door held. As did her spell.

For several too-long minutes, the wind howled against the building, battering it with the force of a hurricane. She kept chanting the spell, over and over, a litany of protection against malevolence. Right when she feared Marco would never leave, the wind died, disappearing as it had come, suddenly and with little warning.

She stepped back until her legs hit the bed and collapsed. Drawing in a deep breath, she tried to still the crazed rhythm of her heart. Several breaths later it finally resumed an almost-normal beat. Now if she could stop her hands from quaking like leaves in a storm.

Was Marco pissed she stayed in his home? Or angry in general? He clearly had issues unrelated to his curse. Whatever his problem, she needed to rid him from the premises. With him present, the apartment would never be safe for guests. Or for her. Sure, she could hide like a frightened child in this room, reinforcing her wards and hoping they held. But where was the fun in that? She wanted to enjoy the Italian summer. To explore the surrounding land. To meet up with Luca.

While able to talk to Luca inside her apartment, she wanted to walk around the estate with him, which wouldn't happen unless she rid the place of Marco.

First, she needed to talk to Luca. He disagreed with

his brother and didn't like the path Marco chose, but disagreement wasn't the same as wanting him banished. Before he stopped by tonight, she would write the banishing spell and ask for permission to use it against his brother.

And hope he didn't hate her for offering.

Chapter Ten

After a shower and an early dinner, Adrianna pulled on a pair of shorts, a T-shirt, and sneakers. Not dressy, but comfortable. And more practical for running if Marco appeared.

She rehearsed the banishing spell in her mind, running over the words, ensuring its potency. Yep. It would work.

Provided Luca gave her permission and Marco appeared again.

A strain of music drifted from the ruins, an orchestra tuning up for an evening concert. She stepped outside, listening to the distance buzz of conversation, to the alluring melodies of Mozart. Luca hadn't mentioned another party, which clearly didn't mean one wasn't happening. He'd said Marco created the parties, but to what purpose? A gathering of fellow ghosts? A way to talk and touch others in the afterlife?

Or was there a more sinister purpose?

If that was the case, why would a cursed evil entity want to create an illusion of a ball, which brought happiness to other spirits?

She had to admit, it was a little fun trying to discover how to free Luca and Marco's purpose in creating parties. Almost like how she first felt when she became a professional medium. The rush of helping people, both living and dead. The thrill of putting together the pieces of conversation snippets to form the entire puzzle of what a spirit tried to communicate.

She missed the feeling of satisfaction.

She left the door unlocked and walked around to where she'd first seen Luca. Except no one leaned against the light brown stone wall. Maybe Marco forgot to tell him about the party.

Right. Even if Marco forgot to mention the ball, Luca had ears.

A touch of icy air brushed against her skin a second before her ghost appeared. Warmth spread across her skin, pooling in her core, as Luca stepped closer.

Adrianna grinned. "Well, hello there."

"Hello." A wrinkle carved a gully between his brows even as his lips curved in welcome. "Would you care to dance?" One arm swept outward to indicate the stairway leading to the tunnel.

Why the worry lines? "I would love to. I didn't realize you were having another party."

Small lines formed around his mouth, edging out from his pressed lips. "Marco decided at the last minute. It will take a while for the guests to appear, but the orchestra has arrived."

"So I hear. They're good."

"They played together before their deaths."

"That's pretty neat they are still playing in death." As well as a little odd a group of musicians continued to play instruments in death instead of passing into the light. Wait until she told Betty about her adventure at the ghost galas. She could almost see the look of disbelief on the older woman's face.

"We are lucky to have them. They have always

played at our parties. Other musicians have attended, but this particular string quartet is the best."

When he paused, she changed the conversation to a more important topic. "Is Marco at the party?"

"Not yet." Luca shook his head. "He is still recovering."

"Recovering?"

His lips turned upward while a sense of pride danced in his eyes. "Whatever you did yesterday still affects him today."

"Not enough for him to leave me alone." Her hands slammed against her hips.

His eyes widened before narrowing into slits. The low timbre of his voice crawled like spiders across her skin. "What do you mean?"

"He chased me from the pool back to the apartment this afternoon." Harshness bit her words even as ice flowed through her veins as she remembered the fierce wind battering the door. "Luckily the wards I placed around the room held, and he couldn't get in."

He cursed. "I am sorry I was not there."

"It is not your job to keep him from attacking me."

He glared, crossing his arms. "You are wrong. I should have expected it and protected you."

Was this an old-fashioned stance of men protecting women? Something standard in his day yet not expected in hers? Or did his protective stance stem from his feelings for her and his desire to protect those he loved?

Did she really just pull out the "L" word?

She drew in a breath and shoved the "L" word into a deep corner of her mind, focusing on the subtext of his words. She understood wanting to protect loved ones. She experienced that emotion often. But the me-man, you-frail-woman approach needed to be nipped in the bud.

"I appreciate you wanting to protect me, but I am capable of protecting myself. Women have to rely upon themselves nowadays, especially where I am from."

He stared at her for a couple of heartbeats before he dropped his arms. "You've proved you can defend yourself. I respect that. But I want to protect you from Marco. You don't know what he's like."

"I'm getting a really good impression. Let's see." She held up her hand, ticking the points off on her fingers. "Evil. Doesn't want me here. And there's something really strange about why he throws these parties."

He leaned his head against the stones, tilting his eyes to the darkening sky. "I've been thinking on that very thing. At first, I truly believed he wanted the company of other spirits besides me. But then something changed. He began to throw these parties with a gleam of pride in his eyes. Not the pride coming from creating an illusion where other ghosts can touch and be touched but pride of purpose. Recently, he's begun to mention how he will seek revenge upon Dario's descendants."

"That's me!" Her eyes widened. "Is that why he attacks me and tells me to leave?"

He shook his head. "He wants you to leave because he enjoys scaring you. I haven't told him you are Dario's great-granddaughter. No, he plans to somehow curse all descendants of Dario's to remain chained to this property and tortured by him. I do not know his plan for obtaining this awful goal. I want nothing to do with it."

She reached for his arm, meaning to give it a little squeeze of solidarity, but her palm passed through to the stones. Drawing back her hand, she sighed. "I know you don't. But you must have some idea of his plan."

A long pause. "I have my suspicions. He will not tell me. But I think he draws energy from the gathering of spirits. He keeps talking about how he's amassing power, and the more he talks of it, the more parties he throws."

She blinked. Since when could spirits gain enough power to do anything with it except move objects? Yes, there were some scary poltergeists who made wind blow inside, moved objects, and terrorized a house's inhabitants, but even they couldn't pull off a stunt as large as Marco and his parties. Maybe if she took another look at the ball, saw past the dancers in their formal dress, skipped over the punch bowl no one drank from, and looked at the construction of the illusion, she might observe what was really happening.

Maybe.

"Let's go dance, Luca. As long as you don't think Marco will show up any time soon?"

He shook his head. "He needs another couple of hours to recover. I am surprised he tried to attack you today. I did not think he left his room."

Bottom line, Marco was stronger than he looked. Something to keep in mind as they attended tonight's ball.

"Come on. I'm looking forward to dancing with you."

He returned her grin as he led her down the stairs.

****

As usual, Luca turned corporeal halfway through the tunnel. Tonight, he created a green grown made of silk. At least it felt like silk to Adrianna. Her experience with centuries-old fashion in Europe was limited to what she'd read in historical romance novels or seen in history books in school. Whatever the material, it felt cool and soft against her skin.

She grabbed his warm hand. Amazing how a stroll through the tunnel changed him into a tangible being, capable of physical contact.

And speaking of physical contact...

He pulled her into an embrace as he swung her onto the dance floor. His smile sent a rush of desire straight to her core. Warmth flooded her limbs as her body pressed against his.

"I enjoy dancing with you."

She ran her hand from his shoulder to his elbow and back. "I feel the same way."

Firm lips brushed against hers, a brief touch before he spun her out and back to his embrace. Yeah, she could get used to dancing with him.

Or more.

Which was nuts. Unless she discovered a way to free him from the curse, their budding relationship was doomed.

A fact she cared less and less about the longer she spent in his embrace. Why not grab the moments with him now instead of worrying about their future?

"Tell me about New York City. I have heard it is quite the place."

She obliged, telling him about the restaurants, Times Square, Broadway, and Central Park until the music ended. She stopped talking as the volume in the room dropped. Breaking her gaze from Luca proved hard, but she used the break between dances to look at the spirits. To really look at them. To see beyond their fancy dresses and tuxedos with tails. Past several centuries' worth of differing hairdos to what lay beneath the surface.

She slapped one hand over her mouth to keep her gasp from escaping.

"What?" Luca's brows pulled into a frown.

She leaned closer, whispering, "Can you look past the spirits' appearances to their souls' auras?"

He glanced, squinting, around the room, before shaking his head. "I cannot."

A small shiver wormed its way through her veins. "Their energies are being siphoned off into the walls. The walls glow with soul energy. That's what Marco is doing, stealing their energy."

He stiffened as he blinked wide eyes. "*Dio Mio*. To hear my suspicions verified..." He shook his head. "He's using the stolen energy to power his spell."

"We have to stop him." And now for the tricky request. What would he do when she asked permission to banish his brother? Give a whoop of delight or shut down her request with an icy glare?

The music started playing another waltz, and after a pause, he swung her into the dance. She swallowed. No biggie. Just ask the question.

"I worked out a banishing spell but wanted your permission before casting it."

His brow wrinkled. "How would you banish him? What would happen to him?"

"Luca"—she met his gaze—"he's evil. I'm sorry to be so blunt, but he's evil."

He glanced over her shoulder, his voice flat with a tinge of sadness. "I know. I've known for years. Where would he go if you banished him?"

What felt like writhing snakes twisted inside her stomach. She swallowed. Now or never. Hopefully he wouldn't throw her out of the ball. "I'd banish him to Hell. Marco's changed enough to be demonic. Evil. And evil spirits should be confined to Hell."

Wide hazel eyes stared at her, although he continued to dance. As if his shocked brain functioned on autopilot, leading her through the dance moves while working through his thoughts.

"Hell?"

Yep, definitely too shocked to form full sentences.

"He can't remain here. On earth. In this mill. Where his powers would grow unchecked until he wreaked havoc on the entire place. He needs to be contained. My spell will send him to Hell. He won't be able to return."

"Have you done this before?" Color returned to his pale cheeks as he spoke.

"Many times." More like a scant few. But who was counting? She knew she could do it again.

"Hell is for sinners."

"And demons." And evil spirits. All points Marco ticked.

"You need my permission?"

"Yes. I do. You are his relative. I won't send him to Hell if you want him around."

He tugged her off the dance floor to a row of dark pink cushioned benches sitting along the wall. He sat beside her, keeping his gaze on their entwined fingers. His thumb stroked back and forth along her palm as emotions ran across his face. She remained quiet, letting him sort his thoughts. At least he wasn't mad at her for asking. But would he make the correct decision? If he said no, would she be able to agree to do nothing?

Maybe she should've thought about that before asking.

"You are correct he needs to be stopped. But to send him to Hell? Is there not another way to help him?"

"I'm not so sure he can be helped. A spirit turns evil in the afterlife if they were evil when alive. He's been bad for a long time." She squeezed his hand. "I'm not going to talk you into something you are against. So when, if ever, you are ready, let me know. Okay?"

As much as she wanted to talk him into giving her the thumbs up to banish Marco, the decision rested on him. As Marco's relative, he needed to give her permission.

He'd come around. She hoped.

He stared at the dancers twirling across the floor. "All right. I'll let you know." His fingers stroked her palm in an absent-minded manner as he continued to stare across the room.

Maybe she should have kept her mouth shut and not asked about the banishing spell. Except Marco's days of roaming the earth needed to end. Sooner rather than later. But she respected Luca's decision.

Although, damn, what was she going to do about Marco if Luca definitely decided against the banishment? How did she bind an evil entity on earth? Banishing was easy. Binding took a lot of energy and experience she lacked.

Asking Luca if she could banish Marco cast a pall

over the evening. He remained quiet, lost in thought, obviously thinking about his brother. Her and her big mouth. She should have waited until the end of the evening, not the beginning to ask.

"I'm sorry." She stroked the back of his hand. "I shouldn't have brought it up."

He shook his head. "No, you were right. Are right. I know you are right, but I cannot yet tell you to do it. Let me think about it." His hazel gaze met hers. "Is there another option?"

Now it was her turn for the head shake. "I'm sorry. I've ruined our evening."

One corner of his lips kicked up. "No. You have stated your mind. I would not want you to hold things in, to feel there is anything you cannot tell me. Even things hard to accept."

She kissed his cheek, a small peck, but he grinned as if she told him she loved him.

Geez, there she went again with the "L" word. What was her deal tonight?

"Thank you. It was not my intent to upset you."

He waved his free hand. "I know. My fears have been realized, and I need time to accept it."

"I'm sorry."

"Enough apologies. Let's dance and enjoy the evening. No more talk of Marco."

Deal. She nodded. He swept her onto the dance floor. Instead of meeting his gaze, she glanced around the room, noticing the spirits' auras still flowed toward the energy-absorbing wall. How did Marco manage that trick? Nothing in her experience as a medium prepared her for seeing ghosts being drained of energy. While she heard of spiritualists draining ghosts to obliterate them, she'd never heard of ghosts doing the same to other ghosts.

Then again, Marco was no more of a ghost than Luca.

What made one brother bad and the other a man she could love? A question asked since humanity first walked the earth.

Stop getting philosophical, Adrianna.

Spending the evening being held by Luca, surrounded by his strong arms, beat thinking about his brother. Marco needed to be banished, and that included removing him from her thoughts for the rest of the evening. *Live in the moment, and tomorrow will take care of itself.*

Luca remained quiet for several more dances, still lost in thought. At least he held her close, touching her as if she were a precious jewel. While a man who tried to protect her from things she could handle drove her nuts, she liked feeling adored.

When the dance ended, his hazel eyes met her gaze. "Would you like to see my room?"

She raised a brow. "Sure! Where is it?"

The tightening of his fingers against hers sent a shot of heat to her core. Warmth spread outward as he led her away from the dancers toward the back of the room. Would he kiss her again? Or did he, like her, desire more?

She glanced at her feet. Yep, they remained on the floor, her slippers peeking from under her skirt with each step. A step landing on the ground. Not a step floating through the air. She swore a layer of air existed between her shoes and the wooden floor.

Funny how an attractive man could create that

feeling in a woman.

Although no other man she'd dated made her feel this way.

Instead of stopping at the painting-covered wall, he tightened his grip on her hand and walked straight through the solid wall. She stiffened, but after her hand and then her arm passed through the wall, she relaxed. Closing her eyes, she stepped through the obvious illusion. She released the breath she'd been holding on the other side. A quick glance over her shoulder showed the ballroom full of people talking, laughing, and dancing. Not a single guest paid them attention. Clearly the illusion prohibited them from seeing farther than the wall.

Light from the ball filtered into the dark corner of the stone cavern, casting their shadows into elongated phantoms creeping along the damp stone walls. Instead of a pleasing fresh-baked cake smell of the ball, this area of the cavern stank like mold and dirt. Probably what the whole place smelled like without the party illusion.

Even more impressive. A magical illusion that masked the cave smell.

Luca glanced over his shoulder, his gaze bouncing between her and the ball. "The illusion does not extend this far."

"I noticed."

"But I can still touch you." Surprise hung in his words.

Adrianna startled. "You mean you didn't know if you'd be able to touch me?"

"I hoped." He gave her hand a little tug as he started walking into the darkening shadows.

She swallowed away the little voice warning her to keep out, to go back to the party where it was safe. But safe was relative. And clinging to the safety of the light taught her nothing. Confidence leaked from Luca's straight posture. He wanted to show her his room, not lead her into a trap.

And she felt safe in his presence.

Small fingers of light flickered around them from the party. She glanced down the hall into the thickening darkness. Ice slipped under her skin. Something lurked in the darkness. Something evil.

"My room is here." The lilt in his voice snapped her attention to him. He had stopped in front of a door. "I will show you my creation. But I warn you, it is not as grand as Marco's."

One quick glance to the stygian darkness—whatever lay back there hadn't moved, thank God—and she winked at Luca.

"Go on. Open the door."

Grinning, he shoved open the door. She made it one step over the threshold, then froze. With the exception of a four-poster bed on the back wall, the place looked like an art museum. Not at all what she'd expected. After a long pause, she stepped inside, walking with the speed of a ninety-nine-year-old, until she stopped in front of a painting.

Wait a minute. She leaned closer. Was that a Renoir?

"You have a Renoir?"

He stepped next to her. "It's an illusion. I created it from memory."

"You have an amazing memory."

Sure, she'd seen the same painting in her college

art class, but remembering it in this amount of detail was impossible. At least for her. Clearly Luca didn't have the same lack of details in his memory. She moved to the next painting and the next, each one bringing another wave of amazement.

"You like art, I see."

A small grin curved his lips. "I do."

She looked at the white marble sculpture of the Madonna and Child. "This is gorgeous. I don't remember seeing it in a museum or art books."

"No. It's a compilation of several sculptures, not an actual one. You could say I created it in more ways than one."

She chuckled. "You did a great job. I'm really impressed. More than impressed. Luca, this is absolutely amazing. Did you use to draw or paint?"

He shook his head. "No. But I loved art. Paintings. Sculptures. Museums. It was a journey to get to the National Roman Museum, and I only went once, but once was enough. I had many art books." He glanced at the nearest painting. "I miss those books."

She stepped past a large, four-poster bed with a thick, red comforter. Not going there, even though she really wanted to hop on the mattress and beckon him closer. What would stop someone at the ball from walking through the stones and interrupting them? Nothing, as far as she could tell. And getting down and dirty in front of a crowd was not in her playbook.

Walking past the bed, she looked at the rest of the paintings. At the last one, she shook her head. "Wow. I'm really impressed."

He reached for her hand, entwining their fingers. "I'm glad you like it." As he pulled her close, his gaze traveled from her eyes to her lips and back as if asking permission.

She wrapped her free hand around his neck, stepped onto her tiptoes, and closed the distance between their lips. His arms tightened around her waist as he deepened their kiss, as his tongue sought and gained entrance to her mouth.

Tingles of desire zipped through her veins, centering in her core. Leaning into him, she tightened her grip on his nape, wishing for fewer clothes between them. The dress was beautiful, but the amount of material prohibited feeling the press of his body against hers.

Which was probably the point of the original design.

Great for nineteenth-century ladies' chastity but not so hot for this twenty-first-century woman who wanted the man before her pressed against her aching body.

The pleasing touch of wandering fingers up her back to her nape sent another round of chills coursing across her limbs. With the speed of a man who knows he has all the time in the world, he unfastened her top button, then the next, and the next. His lips kissed down her neck to her shoulder, giving the skin a little nip. She groaned.

Two could play at this game.

Unlike the slow pace he exhibited, her fingers rushed down the front of his shirt, unbuttoning the buttons as fast as possible. She shoved his shirt open, her lips trailing a path down his neck, over his collarbone. A gasp of air hissed between his teeth.

Ding-dong-ding! Chimes indicating the end of the

ball echoed past her haze of desire. No, no, no. No way was the night already over.

He stepped back, his breath short and fast. He drew in a breath, held it, and released it on a slow exhale, his gaze never leaving hers. She met his eyes, trying to calm her breathing, her racing heart.

"We must go. *You* must go," he said.

"I don't want to."

"I do not want you to either. I want you for the night."

"You can stay the night in my room."

Red tinted his cheeks. "It is not the same."

"I know." Dammit.

"Come now. You must be safe in your apartment before Marco returns." He waved a hand in her direction, and the buttons on her gown fastened.

She raised a brow. "Is that really necessary?"

"Appearances." He passed a hand over his shirt, the buttons fastening on their own.

Nifty trick.

"Come."

She took his extended hand, lacing their fingers, their last touch for the evening. He led her through the transparent, fake wall into the almost-empty cavernous ballroom. Only a few people remained, and those stood in a line to exit. He hauled ass across the room, making it to the tunnel as the last ghost passed inside.

She grabbed her gown, pulling it up so she could match his pace. Halfway through the tunnel, his warm palm turned cold, passing through her hand. Her gown faded away, leaving her clad in a T-shirt and shorts. At least she could run in these clothes.

She hit the stairs at a jog, darting under the arch

and across the grass at a fast pace. Her breath huffed in short gasps as she matched strides with Luca. She forgot how fast ghosts could move. Good thing she wore sneakers and not flip-flops.

Her pace slowed as they reached the graveled patio in front of her apartment. She drew in several gasps of air as she tried to catch her breath. She learned one thing after their dash across the grass. Her exercise schedule needed beefing up.

Light exploded over the mill, igniting the sky with a red-orange pulse of color. A shockwave lanced along the ground like a city snowplow, fast and unyielding.

What the hell? So much for calming her heart rate.

"Hurry!" Luca tried to grab the doorknob, but his hand passed through into the wooden door.

She grabbed the thing, turned it, and shoved open the door. She darted into the apartment, Luca following, and slammed the door shut right as the shockwave hit the apartment. She twisted the lock as the walls of the apartment shook. The lock wouldn't keep out supernatural beings or a demonic pulse of energy, but it made her feel better.

She ran to the window behind the table in time to see the shockwave withdraw into the tunnel. Luckily the apartment held. Not even a stream of dust rained on their heads. Whoever remodeled could add "buildings resist demonic shockwaves" to their résumé.

Luca paced from the fireplace to the kitchenette and back, his footsteps not making a sound. If he had his physical being, he'd be stomping the shit out of the tile.

"What was that light and shockwave?" Although she knew, didn't she? Or at least suspected.

"Marco." He spoke his brother's name in a low growl.

Yep, she was right. Not like it made things better.

She closed the shutters on the window. Like the lock, it really wouldn't do a damn thing against the supernatural, but it made her feel one hell of a lot better.

"This is where he drinks the energy of their souls, isn't it?"

Luca stopped pacing a rut in the tile and shrugged. "I do not know. I have walked with him after parties and been unable to tell what he did. Or how exactly he created the parties. I assume it is like how I create the paintings and sculpture."

"Except you don't use other spirits' energies." A statement. Not a question. She had no doubt in her mind Luca was nothing like Marco.

"No, I use the energy from the surrounding nature. Never another being."

She nodded. What were they going to do about Marco? She promised not to force Luca into allowing her to banish him, but the evil specter needed to be stopped sooner rather than later.

He stepped in front of her. "I will think on what you asked."

"How did you know that's what I was thinking?"

His grin failed to make it to his eyes. "Your emotions play on your face."

"Oh." Good thing she preferred to stick to the truth instead of hiding behind lies.

"Good night, Adrianna."

"I enjoyed the evening." And would like a repeat minus the weird light and creepy-ass blast of energy.

"As did I. Good-bye." Luca disappeared.

She waited a moment, but he didn't return. Neither did Marco. She yawned. The crash of adrenaline weakened her legs, making them wobble like a baby fawn. Time for bed. If Marco failed to get in using hurricane force wind and a shockwave, then her spell would protect her from him while she slept. After a brief stop in the bathroom, she pulled back the covers and crawled into bed. A wave of exhaustion pulled her into unconsciousness.

****

Luca strode to the pool, his shoes not making a sound on the grass. A war raged inside him, indecisions erupting to lay waste to his mind, his soul. Adrianna headed the top of his thoughts. Despite her claiming to be able to protect herself, a need to ensure her safety compelled him to watch her apartment. He sat on the lounger, focusing his gaze on where she slept behind sturdy stone walls.

Any minute his brother would finish drinking the spirits' soul energies and seek him out. He wanted to be seen first thing before Marco got the idea to attack Adrianna again. Oh God, did his brother truly eat spirits' energy like a vampire sucked blood? How could he not have noticed this? How could he have spent over a century in Marco's presence and not noticed what his brother had become?

What was wrong with him?

Well, at least he knew the answer to his question. He spent years, over a century, admiring his brother. His beloved brother. Who was no longer beloved.

But to banish him to Hell? Was Marco truly that evil?

Yes, he is.

Damn little mind voice.

He might not like it, but the little mind voice spoke true. Knowing the truth and acting on it, though, remained two separate things. Could he tell Adrianna to banish his brother?

Would banishing Marco harm her? Luca shook his head. She said she'd banished spirits before, and she was fine. If she was hurt, it would devastate him.

Somehow, during the last few days, he'd fallen for the American woman. Fallen hard. The feelings she woke in him ran deeper than anything he had ever experienced. He wanted her with him for life.

As if that could happen in his current state. First, he needed to find freedom from his curse. But in order to do so, he must tell Adrianna her role in the matter. At least what he thought her role might be since he had no exact idea how to obtain freedom.

A ray of light broke free of the horizon, casting a beam on the mill, highlighting the brown stones into a glow of beauty. Until a dark shadow shot out of the collapsed ceiling of the ruined wing to land on the grass, rolling in a loose ball toward him.

He stiffened as Marco approached. The shadow coalesced on the opposite side of the pool, dissolving into the shape of a man. The smile on his brother's lips offered more fear than comfort. He stood.

"You look well, Marco."

A lie. Evil never looked well.

"As do you, brother. I see you enjoyed the party."

"Where were you?"

The smile fled from Marco's face, leaving behind reddened cheeks and a snarl. "Recovering. The bitch staying here hurt me badly. Where were you when I needed you?"

"You were recovering on your own. What did you need me for? You've amassed enough power in the cavern to heal yourself."

Marco's eyes widened. "Ah. You have learned my secret. You finally opened your eyes. Good. You know I will use the stored energy to destroy Dario's descendants."

"I am tired of your destroying talk." He slashed a hand through the air. "Leave them be and get over it."

"Get over it? Dario ruined my life. Ruined yours. How can you say to get over it? That is madness, brother." Marco glanced to Adrianna's apartment. A gleam shone in his eye when he turned back. "Or have you fallen for the woman? Ah, you have. She is worthless and will soon leave this place. Then where will you be?"

"In a better place than you."

"Is that all you have, brother? You are pathetic. Very well. If you don't want to participate in eliminating Dario's descendants, then I will do it myself. Just like I would have done anyway."

"You leave them alone. They don't deserve what you have planned."

Marco *tsked*. "Luca, Luca, Luca. I grow weary of you. If you weren't the only consistent person for me to talk with over the century, I would have done away with you long ago. You are weak. Not worthy of the Fausto name."

Rage shot through him, obliterating the ache Marco's words left in his chest. Fists balled, he glared at the creature who used to be his beloved brother. "I am more worthy than you. My soul is not tainted with the filth of murder and the stain of revenge. Cursed I am, but only because I stood beside you. Why do you think Dario gave us a way out of the curse? Because he felt sorry for you?" His palm slapped against his chest. "No! He felt sorry for me. He realized I should not have been there. You were the target of his curse, not me. You, Marco. You and your evil ways."

For a brief moment, Marco stared open-mouthed at him. But only for a moment before he threw his head back, laughing like a possessed demon. "That may be, but cursed you are, and cursed you shall remain, for all of Dario's descendants will die."

The evil peal of laughter trailed behind as slithering fingers of darkness enveloped him into a dense ball of shadows. The ball rolled across the grass to disappear into the inky depths of the tunnel.

Luca heaved in several deep breaths as the creature disappeared. Tension drained from his muscles although his head continued to pound. Little sparks of red danced around the periphery of his vision, receding from view the more air he sucked down.

He stared at the path Marco took back to the mill. Thank God he'd left Adrianna alone. For now. How long would it take him to realize she was one of Dario's descendants? What would he do to her once he learned her ancestry?

He swallowed. Protect the woman he loved or save a brother who was beyond saving? A small shiver snaked its way through his veins, a cold shock of truth.

When Adrianna woke, he would agree to what she wanted.

Marco's banishment.

Chapter Eleven

Adrianna woke with a start, her dream dissipating like steam over water in the light of dawn. A couple of deep breaths later and she rolled to a sit. Whatever her dream was about, it left behind a sense of dread.

She ran a hand over her face. As much as she enjoyed her time spent with Luca, she was getting too old for staying up all night every night. Sad, but true. Not that the knowledge would stop her from spending time with him.

After a quick dash through the shower, she dressed in a pair of shorts, T-shirt, and sneakers. If none of her psychic friends could devise a way to free Luca from his curse, then she was on her own. And the first thing she needed to do was discover exactly how Marco leached energy from the souls of the dead.

Although if she was being truthful with herself, wanting to learn Marco's tricks had less to do with learning how to free Luca and more about attaining information on cursed spirits and their capabilities.

In case she ever decided to return to being a medium.

The idea no longer sounded as scary as when she'd first arrived in Italy.

After stuffing her phone in her pocket, she grabbed the flashlight from the nightstand and headed out the door. Her apartment would be safe from Marco since her spell held him at bay, keeping him from crossing the threshold, which totally pissed off the evil spirit.

Except all his anger had to go somewhere, and the probability it would be reflected back on her was high. Which meant she needed a binding spell until Luca allowed her to banish Marco.

If he allowed her to banish Marco.

She sighed. Banishing worked so much better than binding. Especially since she had no experience in binding an evil spirit. Zippo. None.

Clearly it was time she learned.

Marco would only grow worse as the years passed. What if he turned on Luca? She could not, would not allow that to happen. The ghost had crept into her heart, setting up residence as if she'd known him her entire life. Forever. A form of completeness she had never felt with another man.

And yet he remained a cursed spirit. Cursed never to age. To watch from afar. Never to leave her family's ancestral lands.

If she wanted this relationship to last, she needed to free him. Hell, she'd want to free him even if she hadn't fallen hard for him. He didn't deserve the life forced upon him, didn't deserve to be cursed into spirit form forever.

So hell yeah, she was going to free him.

Once she figured out how.

She strode across the grass to the ruined wing. For now, she wanted to check out the ballroom in the light of day—or by flashlight, as the case may be—and see if she noticed anything different about the place when it wasn't cloaked in illusion.

Besides the obvious difference of stone hewed

walls unadorned with tapestries and paintings.

She passed where she first saw Luca leaning against the wall. Her fingers touched the sun-warmed stone. As she drew closer to the arched stairway, a sense of malevolence passed through her, a warning to stay away. A huge, metaphysical Keep-Out sign for humans. The same feeling had passed through her on her first day here when she explored the mill but had eased when she walked with Luca through the tunnel. The last couple of nights, she hadn't felt it at all.

But it was back in full force now.

Click. She pressed the button on the flashlight, shining the beam down the stairs into the darkness of the tunnel. She shivered.

Nothing to it. You've walked this before. You can walk it again.

Taking a deep breath, she stepped onto the stone stair. One step, two, and then she was in a rhythm, treading as softly as possible, the flashlight held in front of her like a weapon. She swept the beam back and forth, pointing it into the tunnel.

Was she actually going to enter a tunnel haunted by an evil entity? Judging by the fact her feet kept moving forward, the answer to that question was a resounding yes. Hopefully this "adventure" wouldn't be like the dumb female lead in a horror movie, chasing a noise into the basement when she knew good and well a serial killer lurked about.

The tunnel seemed longer than she remembered, no doubt a product of her imagination coupled with a steady dose of adrenaline. She released a breath she hadn't known she held when she stepped into the large room.

Sweeping the beam of the flashlight in an arc, she looked around the room. Nothing in it resembled a ballroom. Water dripped from rough-hewn walls, running in brown rivulets to the stone floor. Moss grew on some of the stones. A constant *drip-drip-drip* sounded from the back of the room, and she pointed her light toward the noise. Nothing obvious popped out. No large running streams, only the slight echo of dripping water.

Which was as annoying as hell.

The noise crept down her spine with gouging fingernails, torturing her nerves. Light from her flashlight shimmied along the wall as her hand shook. Clearly the thing weighed too much. It wasn't like she was actually scared.

Right?

Sure, Adrianna. The things you tell yourself.

She drew in a deep breath. *Come on. You've done this before.*

Okay, not exactly like this, but she had banished an evil spirit, one who was almost as mean as Marco. Although the experience didn't involve entering a creepy-ass tunnel leading to an underground cavern with an annoying-as-hell drip from nowhere. But still. She'd done it before. She could do it again.

Steadying her hand, she stepped closer to the nearest wall, peering at the stones. Once she relaxed, after a couple of deep breaths, she saw the energy lines, a tangle of strands woven into a pulsing power. She placed a hand against the wall, gasping as the power thrummed through her veins.

What was Marco planning to do with all this raw energy? How did he manage to store it? What had given him the idea in the first place?

She walked toward the back of the cavern, letting her hand stroke against the wall. Her fingers tingled from the power, but she left it alone, not daring to draw it into herself, to use the ill-gained energy. Best to leave it where it hung on the wall like macabre strands of tinsel.

Damp permeated her clothes. Or maybe that was fear-sweat. Nope. Couldn't be. She was not afraid.

Fake it till you make it.

Shadows played along the wall, creeping alongside in time with her steps.

It's just shadows, Adrianna. Nothing but shadows.

Shadows and stored up stolen energy, that was. Nothing to fear.

Light bounced off a familiar slash in the stone wall. The passageway to Luca's room. She swallowed. What were the chances he was there? She took a step forward, then paused. A noise like footsteps sounded toward the entrance of the room. The pounding of her heart echoed in her ears as she pointed the beam of light toward the noise.

"Hello?"

Water *drip-drip-dripped* an answer. Grabbing the flashlight with both hands, she pointed the thing toward the entrance. Just her luck, the beam stopped before it reached the tunnel. Great. Someone could be standing swathed in the shadows where the tunnel met the cavern. She took a step closer, sweeping the light back and forth. Was someone hiding? Watching her stumble in the dark armed with only a flashlight? Yet another thought to send her heart into palpitations.

She'd almost rather face the New York paparazzi

than walk through a dark cave. *Almost*.

"Adrianna?"

Letting loose a squeak, she jumped, dropping her flashlight. The beam careened over the wall, flickering like a strobe as the flashlight rolled across the ground.

"Sorry." Strong hands grabbed her upper arms.

Luca.

She sagged against him, her back to his chest, and practiced breathing like an average human, one hand pressed against her chest. Maybe if she pressed hard enough, her heart would stop imitating the speed of a hummingbird's wings.

"You about scared me to death." She turned to face him. The dim light etched sharp shadows across his cheeks.

Wide eyes searched hers as he laid his hand on her arm. "I can touch you."

"So I noticed. Which is why you about scared me to death." Wait a minute. He touched her outside of the ball.

"I'm sorry."

"You touched me!" she said at the same time.

Both of them stared at each other for a pause.

"How—?"

"Why—?"

She laughed, adrenaline subsiding with a rush of humor. The situation wasn't funny, but she continued chuckling, laughter a release valve for her nerves. Luca raised a brow. A small grin cracked his lips.

"Sorry." She bent and picked up the flashlight, pointing the beam at her feet.

"No, I am sorry for scaring you. It was not my intent."

"I know." She placed a tentative hand on his arm. His physical arm. "How are you solid? I thought it only happened at the parties."

"Me too. And yet when I saw you and reached out, I could touch you." His eyes narrowed. "What are you doing here?"

"I wanted to see if I could discover how Marco stole energy from the spirits. I've never met a ghost who could do that." She pointed her light at the nearest wall. "The walls are a repository for the spirits' energies."

"The energy is stored in this room?" He stepped closer to the wall and placed his fingertips on the damp stone.

"Yes. Can you feel it?"

"A little. Is seeking out this energy the only reason you walked in here?"

He shook his hand as he faced her, as if the tingle of power bothered him more than he wanted to admit.

"I'm not so much seeking out the energy as trying to figure out how he does it." Her gaze met his. "I hoped by learning his trick I could discover a way to free you from the curse." She swallowed. "So I really came here for you."

Wide hazel eyes stared at her. Great. After kissing him last night and the way he reacted to her, she thought he'd be more happy than surprised. Surely he knew she found him attractive. Her face heated. Maybe she'd made a mistake in expressing how she felt.

His teeth gleamed white in the shadows, slashing lines across his face. "For me? You braved the spell designed to keep out the living to help me?"

Clearly not a mistake. Her palm brushed against

the stubble lining his cheek. "Always."

She touched her lips to his warm ones. His arms wrapped around her waist, drawing her closer, pressing her against his warmth. Without the extra fabric of a ball gown between them, she felt the small shifts of his body rubbing against hers. Fire pumped through her veins, her core tingling as she deepened their kiss. Good thing he held her since her knees forgot their purpose and wobbled like a newborn colt, incapable of holding her weight.

She pulled back in a futile attempt to gain control. Aw, hell. Who was she kidding? Gaining control while around him ranked at the top of her not-gonna-happen list. Why bother? Giving in was a helluva lot more fun.

"Why don't we move this to your room?"

Not the best pickup line ever, but not the cheesiest either. And judging by the way his eyes flared, it hit the mark.

****

Luca's heart pounded a staccato beat. The husky tone of Adrianna's voice stroked him as surely as if she'd clasped him in her hand. Did she mean what he thought, he hoped? He swallowed. But in case she didn't, he asked, "You want to see the paintings?"

"No." Red tinted her cheeks as she shook her head. Even in the dim light he saw the high color. "I mean, yes, they're gorgeous, but no, I want to see you."

She meant what he hoped. Not bothering to hide his grin, he grabbed her hand. Skin against skin. Warmth streamed from her palm into his, a pleasing balm for his soul. At long last, Mother Mary listened and allowed him to touch the woman he loved.

Another swallow. Love? Dare he say the word?

Shut up, Luca, and take her to bed.

Now that little mind voice had the right idea.

"I would love to show you my room. Again. When no partygoers are around." He waggled his brows.

Her body relaxed as she grinned. "That would be nice. Public displays of affection really aren't my thing."

"Nor mine." He tugged her hand as he walked backward a couple of steps toward his room. "Come. You can see how I've changed the artwork."

More like how he'd changed the bed. When he lived, his bed had been small. When he created his room, he'd needed a part of his past, something to remind him of home. For years the bed served that purpose. But with Adrianna coming into his life, he'd wished for something different, larger than he used to own. His creation last night had seemed to please her. Since she liked the oversized thing, he'd kept the four posters with the glaring red cover.

As an extra benefit, the larger bed gave them more space to move than the smaller one he used to sleep on before the curse.

He shoved open the door, waved a hand to create a different look, and let her walk through first. Dropping her hand, he closed the door and drew in a deep breath. It had been a while for him. A long while. Sex with spirits left much to be desired, even when they both possessed physical bodies.

Candles flickered from a hundred glass holders set around the room and in brackets on the wall. Illusionary, but effective in giving the room a soft glow. Women liked romantic lights, soft shimmers like a roomful of candles. At least that's what the television claimed.

"Wow." Adrianna took a couple of steps, turning in a slow circle. "This is gorgeous."

Yes! His last-second idea worked.

He stepped closer to her, a rush of nerves running beneath his skin mixed with an expanding desire. She paused, clicked off the hand torch she carried, and dropped it onto the carpeted floor as she pressed her body against his. He wrapped his arms around her waist and pressed his lips against her soft ones.

Heaven. Pure heaven.

Her hands trailed from his nape to his collarbone, fingers working the buttons on his shirt until he shrugged it onto the floor. Backing toward the bed, she yanked her shirt over her head. He followed her, his fingers lightly touching the lace of her bra.

"We didn't have these in my day."

"Shut up and come here."

He obeyed, drinking in her kiss, her desire as he followed her down onto the bed. Her skin tasted salty as he licked his way from her neck, over the firm globe of her breast, to the lace bra. Pretty, but how did he remove it without appearing addled?

As if she read his mind, she wiggled until she was able to unfasten the thing. A shrug later and she tossed the bra onto the floor. He returned her smile before pulling her nipple into his mouth, teasing it with his tongue. His hand pinched her other nipple, rolling it between thumb and finger in time to the pulsing of his tongue until she rewarded him with a moan.

She clasped his head against her breast, her hips moving against his, rubbing his cock against her core. One hand trailed across the soft skin of her stomach until he reached the waistband of her shorts.

He raised his head from her breast. "You're overdressed for the occasion."

"Speak for yourself." She sat, unfastened her shorts, and shoved them and her panties off.

He quickly shed his pants, lay back on the bed, and pulled her into his arms. Her hand fisted around his cock, stroking him up and down, up and down. If she didn't stop, he'd explode before he made it inside her.

Firm lips covered his, her tongue stroking in rhythm to her hips. He ran a hand down her spine to her bottom. Peering up at her from lowered lids, he placed his hands under her ass and lifted. She took the silent hint, straddled his hips, and guided him inside. A moan escaped her lips when he slid into the welcoming grasp of her wet core. Her warmth enveloped him, held him close, as he sank his soul into hers.

"You feel good." Her whisper against his neck sent a shiver coursing through his limbs.

"So do you."

Then she began to move, and he felt like his world tilted, shifted, until he lost all sensation of their separate bodies, only aware of the pleasure coursing through his soul.

And when their heavy pants relaxed, he held her close, pulling her against his body, into his heart, and swore never to let her go. No matter what happened, she belonged to him. While he was the one cursed, she possessed his heart, and God help him if he failed to protect her.

She was his.

All right, Luca. You might want to ease up a bit. She already stated she didn't need your protection.

True. But he couldn't help the way he felt.

She ran a hand down his chest. "That was nice."

"Just nice?"

She grinned. "By nice I mean, you were great, I loved it, and how soon do you want to do it again?"

A smile spread across his face. "Again? Already?"

"Always."

All right, then. He kissed her, sinking into her body, wrapping his soul around her heart, vowing to keep her with him forever.

****

After round—what was it again? Three? Four?—Luca lay on his back, Adrianna snuggled against his side. Peace coursed through him, a relaxation he had not experienced since the curse cast him into this half life.

A peace not likely to last if he continued to hide from her how he needed her in order to break his curse. Yes, she had stated she would help free him. She even braved the spell over the tunnel in order to help him find a way to freedom.

But neither of those actions meant she would be all right with his omission about her role in freeing him. He'd led her to believe a spell existed. Words spoken aloud that broke his curse. A simple way to reverse what had been done to him once the correct words were known. He failed to mention as a descendant of Dario, she was needed to free him from the curse. Not a spell she cast. Not discovering how Marco drank the soul energy of the spirits. Her. Adrianna.

He could perform selfless acts for all eternity, but without her, all the good he achieved was for naught.

He needed to tell her sooner rather than later. And

hope she would not be angry.

Rolling over, Luca faced her. "I need to tell you something."

Small, warm fingers drew a path along his collarbone. Chill bumps rose on his skin, tracing a line straight to his cock, which rose to the occasion. He shook his head, trying to gain control of an involuntary reaction. Which failed. His gaze dropped to her hand on his skin. Would she still want him once he told her?

Her fingers paused. "What is it? You seem serious."

"I didn't tell you everything."

She stiffened, her fingers pausing their exploration. "What do you mean?"

"About my curse. I left out something important."

"Okay. What?"

He swallowed. Now or never. His words escaped his lips in a rush. "When Dario cursed us, he gave us an out. He said to be free from the curse we must perform a selfless act upon one of his descendants. You are his descendant. In order for me to be free from the curse, I must help you somehow. But I don't know what he meant by a selfless act. I've tried to help out Maria and Luigi, but nothing happened. I'm still cursed."

Her hand dropped from his chest. "Was all this"—she waved between them—"just some ruse to win your freedom?"

"No! I care for you." Hell, he loved her, but now was not the time to mention that particular emotion.

"It sounds to me like you used me to free yourself." She rolled over, threw back the covers, and sat on the edge of the bed. "I planned on helping you. You didn't have to sleep with me for that to happen."

What felt like a pile of rocks expanded against his stomach, pressing into a painful knot. He swallowed. He hurt her. God knew, he would never hurt her on purpose, but his omission caused her pain as surely as if he hit her. "I know. And I'm thankful. I want to be truthful. I want you to know your part in my curse."

"And you couldn't have mentioned this earlier?" She stood and yanked her clothes off the floor—each item a little stab to his heart—and pulled them on while talking. "Why didn't you say anything?"

"I was afraid." Of her reacting the way she was. Of her anger. "I thought you'd leave me."

"Leave you?" She sucked in a breath as if counting to ten. "You were afraid if you told me the truth, I wouldn't help you?"

"Yes." Summed up like that, his reasoning sounded stupid.

"I would have helped you no matter what. You don't deserve to be cursed. But I don't deserve to be lied to."

She stood at the foot of the bed, arms crossed, feet wide apart like an avenging warrior. Luca pressed his lips together to keep off the grin. She made him happy. Even when he was not sure if she would walk out of the room or stay with him.

Definitely not a smiling matter.

A shadow flickered by the door, drawing his attention off Adrianna. He squinted. Flickering candles might produce a romantic vibe, but the dim light they produced prohibited a clear view. He leaned to the side to see if the shadow was a concern or a trick of the shimmering light.

She leaned in the same direction and waved her

148

hands. "Hello? Luca?"

His breath froze in his lungs as the shadow grew. Elongated fingers stretched across the walls, reaching toward Adrianna. Oh, Madonna save them.

"Look out!"

She turned at his shout. He grabbed the sheet to throw it off him and leap from the bed. His feet brushed the floor when a blast of light slammed into him, knocking him against the headboard. Black spots flickered in his periphery as he struggled to stay conscious. The shadow wrapped around Adrianna, choking off her scream. He tried to move, to stand, to save the woman he loved. But another blast of light engulfed him, and he succumbed to a suffocating darkness.

Chapter Twelve

Adrianna woke to a headache and what felt like a hard rock pressing into her stomach. No, not a rock. A shoulder. She hung upside down, looking at a man's backside as he carried her. The feeling of evil slithered across her skin, wrapping her in its cold embrace. Oh shit. Only one person she knew exuded a malevolent aura. What happened? Where was Luca? Where was she? Darkness surrounded them, making it impossible to determine where she was being taken. Although she was pretty sure they remained underground, walking through a twisting labyrinth of passageways stemming from the main cavernous room. Hard to tell in the almost-nonexistent light, but it looked like stone walls and floors.

Her lungs forgot their purpose, freezing air from passing through her lips, and she forced the things to inhale a breath. No sense in giving away her conscious status to the demonic entity who'd slung her over his shoulder like a dead body.

How had he captured her? The last she remembered was talking to Luca. More like arguing with him for lying to her. Well, not really lying, although one could make an argument hiding the truth was a form of lying. Whatever the distinction, annoyance had rocked her core. And it hadn't helped when he leaned to the side as if his wall art was more interesting than hashing things out with her.

Dumbass. He wasn't looking at the paintings. He was trying to see who or what walked in the room. But how was she supposed to have known he wasn't trying to avoid the conversation?

The person he saw managed to pull a fast one, capturing her and carrying her off like a stolen bride.

One minute they were arguing and the next, well, remembering what came next proved hard. How had he captured her? And where was Luca?

Shards of ice snaked through her veins. Was Luca dead? Could a cursed spirit die?

The hand holding her legs released its grip, and she dropped onto a crinkly mattress with a gasp. She squinted in the sudden light, crab-walking in a mad scramble until her back hit damp stones.

Marco stood before her, surrounded by a cloud of shadows. Cold waves of malice pulsed against her skin. Black eyes glared at her as his lips pulled into a parody of a smile.

"Ah. You are awake."

Yeah, you asshole. She glared.

"Welcome to my room." His arms swept out from his body as if inviting her to take a look.

A quick glance showed walls bare of decoration. Iron brackets with flickering flames hung in intervals around the small room. Despite their light, shadows crept along the stone floor like roaches looking for a meal. The straw-stuffed mattress, which lay thrown on the floor like a discarded toy, rustled as she moved.

Other than the hiss and crackle of the torches, the only other sound she heard was her pulse thudding an echo in her ears.

She focused her gaze on him. Best to keep her full attention on the threat.

He laughed, the noise raking fingernails down her spine. Tension tightened her limbs.

"You should never have ventured to our domain. We rule down here." He leaned forward and stabbed a finger at her. "You are nothing, and I cannot have my brother distracted by you. He's had his fun. Now you must die."

"Why not kill me where you found me?" Amazing. Her voice sounded normal despite the tremors racing through her.

An imitation of a smile stretched his lips, baring his teeth. "You've been an annoyance to me. Living here. Hurting me. You must pay first. Luca enjoyed you. Perhaps I will too."

Yeah, not happening, buddy.

Her eyes narrowed as she pressed a shaky hand against the damp stone and used the wall as a crutch to stand. Cowering on a dirty mattress gave the appearance of weakness. And if he thought she was going to scream in fear instead of escape his clutches, he had another think coming.

Up next on a short agenda: escape this room, find Luca, and ensure Marco never hurt another person, living or dead.

Calming her adrenaline-charged pulse, she drew in a deep breath, pulling energy from the ground, centering her thoughts. Power rushed into her faster than when she'd defeated Marco at the pool, as if the stored spirits' energy wanted to help her defeat the demonic bastard.

Marco shook his head. "Why fight me? You know

I'm stronger."

Sure you are. That's why I kicked your ass the other day.

She kept the thought to herself, not giving him the victory of a response. By remaining silent, she hoped to draw out his anger. Angry people made mistakes. Angry spirits too.

Instead she focused on gathering as much energy as possible, focusing the power into her palms. Her grandfather's ring grew warm with a gentle pulse of heat.

Weird. It had never felt like anything other than skin-warmed metal until now. Why the sudden change?

A topic for later. After she escaped. Checking out the jewelry instead of focusing on the upcoming fight was the epitome of stupidity.

Marco glanced at her hand, and his eyes widened. He pointed at the ring, a fine tremor shaking his finger. "You wear Dario's ring."

His comment snapped her attention to the ring. The stone glowed a deep red.

What the hell?

She held up her hand, palm facing him. *Get out first. Think about the ring later.* "So?"

He snarled. "I'm going to kill you. Dario tried to kill me, and you wearing his ring means you are a descendant of his. You deserve to die, and I'm the weapon making it happen."

His snarl turned into a yell as he leapt forward. Focusing on the ring, she channeled the accumulated power straight into Marco. A beam of light slammed into him midleap, throwing him against the opposite wall. Like at the pool, he shifted between a physical state and a transparent one as he slid down the wall to rest splay-legged on the floor. His head lolled to the side.

Dammit. One of his legs blocked her path out the open door. Keeping her eyes on Marco, she sidled toward him. He remained still. Taking a deep breath, she stepped over his leg. He didn't notice. Air rushed from her lungs as her heart thudded a crazed rhythm. Time to get the hell out of here.

Which way to go? A quick glance to the left showed a stone wall. Right it was. She took off running, sprinting as fast as she could to get away from him. But the light from his room only lasted a dozen feet. Unless she wanted to risk tumbling down an unknown flight of stairs, falling into a hole, or tripping over uneven stones, she needed to slow to a more reasonable pace.

Her heart pounded a beat that echoed in her ears. Breath sawed in and out of her lungs. If she didn't get things under control soon, he could follow her by sound alone.

Touching her fingers against the wall, she crept into the darkness. How far did this passage go? Forever? Where was Luca? Was he still alive? Or as alive as a ghost could be?

She sucked in a breath. *Calm down, breathe deep. Don't freak, don't freak, don't freak.*

Self-talk got her all of nowhere fast.

She was not going to die. Not happening. Not here. Not now. Once she calmed down—which was totally going to happen at any moment—she could try the banishing spell. Or set the same spell protecting her apartment around herself.

A little hard to do while trying to escape an

enraged entity.

Her fingers ran along the rough-hewed stone. Sharp breaths punctuated each step as breath heaved in and out of overworked lungs. Had she moved fast enough to escape the demon's clutches? A small sound drifted through the passage, like a physical strike from behind. A groan. Marco. Shuffling footsteps echoed against the stone.

Shit, shit, shit.

As if someone flicked on a light switch, a dull glow began to emanate from the stones. Not bright, but enough to see by. Enough to see holes or stairs. Energy pulsed under her fingers, the stolen soul energy of the spirits lighting her way. She picked up her pace until she darted along the passageway as fast as she dared.

She turned a corner, and light streamed across the stone floor of the passageway. Running, she headed straight for the slash of light.

And right into Luca.

A little squeak escaped her lips as he grabbed her upper arms. Relief coursed through her at his touch.

"You're okay!"

"What happened?" Their words crashed into one another as they spoke simultaneously.

Before she could answer, running footsteps echoed against the stones. Luca shoved her behind him into his room and stepped into the passageway.

"Marco!"

She followed Luca out of his room. No way was she cowering inside while he handled things.

Marco stepped into the light, his features becoming clearer the closer he came. Rage wrapped around him like a cloud of death. Black eyes flashed in a face carved from the depths of Hell. One finger pointed at her.

And when he spoke, his voice warped the surrounding air. "She belongs to Dario. What are you doing with her?"

"Leave her alone, Marco." Luca faced his brother, fists knotted at his side. "Leave them all alone. I know what you are up to, how you steal the spirits' energies."

Marco slashed a hand through the air. "It matters not. They are dead."

"You are stealing their souls! How can that not matter?" Luca shook his head. "Never mind. You do not care."

"Ah, yes, brother. On that you are correct. They are merely a means to an end. The endgame being to kill all of the descendants of Dario. Starting with this one."

Marco touched the wall, drawing the same energy into his body that had lit Adrianna's path. With a loud yell, he threw the energy at her, a bolt of light shooting from his palm.

Eyes wide, frozen in place, she stared at the streaming bolt of death.

Luca shoved her out of the way. She slammed into the stone wall, her shoulder screaming in pain. The bolt of energy struck Luca in the upper chest, blowing him backward to land in an unmoving sprawl of limbs. She pushed off the wall, running to where he lay upon the cold, damp stone floor.

"Luca!" She knelt by his side.

His eyes rolled, lids flickering open. "Banish. Do it." His fingers moved as if searching for hers. She grasped his hand as his eyes closed.

She laid a hand on his chest, watching and feeling

for any sign of life, but he remained still, no longer drawing in breaths. Was he dead? Or did the cursed control their breathing around the living, and he was only unconscious?

Either way, Marco was about to meet his final fate.

"This is an unfortunate outcome."

She jumped at Marco's voice by her side. So focused on Luca, she'd forgotten to track the demonic creature's location. Bad move.

Except Luca had given her permission to banish his brother. All she needed to do was calm herself, set up a protective circle, and cast the spell. No problem.

She suppressed the maniacal laughter threatening to escape her lips. No problem? Right.

Marco shoved her to the side and knelt beside his brother. She shuffled backward, sneakers shoving into the ground, palms scraping against the uneven stone, as she tried to escape his reach. An unneeded move since Marco touched Luca's arm, bowing his head in a grotesque parody of prayer and atonement. Like any prayer out of his mouth would work. Her movements went unnoticed by Marco and gave her the distance needed to focus on her banishing spell.

Drawing in several deep breaths, she centered her thoughts, sinking her energy into the ground, seeking and finding a responding energy to help power her spell. An imaginary circle surrounding her appeared in her mind, glowing bright gold with power. She pictured banishing runes on her palms and faced her palms toward Marco.

His head snapped to her. A snarl ripped across his lips. "Bitch! You killed him!"

Right. Because she was the one who'd shot the

deadly bolt of energy.

Thoughts she kept to herself as she focused on the power surrounding her, power fueling her spell, power running through her and out her palms.

"If Marco threatens me in this place,
Fight Water by Water and Fire by Fire."

Eyes wide, Marco lunged at her, but the circle held, not allowing him entrance. He roared, shifting into his shadow form, trying to break past her defenses.

She swallowed, speaking the rest of the spell in a rush while he continued battering against the energy of the circle.

"Banish his soul into nothingness,
And remove his powers until the last trace.
Let this evil being flee,
Through time and space.
With this spell, I banish thee straight to Hell!"

White light streamed from her palms, slamming into the shadow, knocking Marco into human form. The warped timbre of his scream vibrated against the stones, raining dust particles upon her head.

White light continued to pour from her palms into him as tiny cracks of light slashed through his skin. His screams grew louder as the slashes of light joined together. An explosion of sparks silenced his yell as he disappeared into Hell's dark depths.

She dropped her arms, slumping forward, gasping for air. The spell drained her of energy, in more ways than one, but since dirt continued to drop like heavy rain, she needed to get the hell out of the cavern. Lack of energy be damned.

Standing on shaking legs, she stepped to Luca, grabbed his heavy body under the arms, and dragged him into the main cavern. Small stones rained upon her head as if banishing Marco had caused instability of the structure. Hopefully the place would hold. After five centuries, she would have thought banishing a demonic spirit would not affect the mill's structural integrity, but it looked like she was wrong.

Raining stones drowned out the echoes of the dripping water that had annoyed her earlier. What she wouldn't give for some irritating little drips instead of the steady *plunk-plunk-plunk* of dirt and small rocks. She glanced over her shoulder, not yet seeing the tunnel entrance. Gods, how much farther? Sure, she could get out faster if she wasn't dragging Luca, but no way could she leave his body behind. She would drag him through the tunnel as far as he remained a physical being, as far as possible. If this cavern collapsed, she refused to allow him to be buried. He deserved a real grave next to his family, not to be buried under a pile of rocks in the place where he'd spent the last century trapped.

Keeping the wall to her right and checking every few steps with her foot it was still there, she kept heading toward the tunnel. One step, two steps, three steps, four steps, check the wall. Keep going. Her breath came in large pants, her arms ached, and her back hurt. If she got out of this alive, she'd spend more time at the gym.

Not much farther, Adrianna. Keep going. Hustle your butt or die. Dying wasn't on the agenda. Getting the hell out of a collapsing cavern was.

Light trickled through the falling dust. She stopped and turned. *Hallelujah!* The tunnel entrance stood about six feet to her left. Leaving the wall, she moved as fast as possible toward the light. With a burst of adrenaline, she dragged Luca faster, not pausing as his feet cleared the entrance to the tunnel.

Halfway through the tunnel, the dirt stopped falling, and she breathed a sigh of relief. They burst through the tunnel into the landing before the arched flight of steps. Since dirt no longer fell and the ground remained steady, she lowered him to the ground in front of the stairway and sat beside him, catching her panting breath. Why was he still corporeal? Usually at this point in the structure, he turned into a ghost, transparent and unable to be touched.

Yet he remained solid. She stroked the hair off his forehead and dusted the dirt and small stones from his body. Tears formed in her eyes, warping her view into a wavy mirage. He gasped. Tears might cloud her vision, but they did nothing to block her hearing. What the hell? She dashed her fingers across her eyes.

"Luca?" She shook his shoulder. Was he alive? How could he be alive? "Luca?"

Another gasp followed by a cough. He rolled to his side, coughing a few more times. One palm touched the ground, fingers splayed. Tentative at first, he then slapped his hand against the rough stone.

"Luca!" Grabbing his arm, she rolled him to face her. "You're alive!"

Pesky tears wavered in her eyes again, but this time they had nothing to do with sorrow. She scrubbed a hand under her eyes and grabbed him in a hug. Warmth flowed from his body into hers. Warmth. He lived.

But how?

She drew back, her gaze searching his. The large vein on the side of his neck pumped a rhythm. Air flowed in and out of his lungs. Like a living person. Her hands shook as warm tingles spread throughout her body.

He lived.

He reached out a hand to touch her face. "I'm no longer in the cavern. How can I touch you?"

"I don't know. Can you walk? Are you okay? I thought you died. I guess a cursed spirit doesn't die?"

He shook his head as she helped him sit. "Where's Marco?"

She touched his cheek. "I banished him. You gave me permission." But was he mad?

"Good. He was no longer my brother. He'd turned into a demonic creature I no longer recognized. I realized it before you came looking for me." His gaze dropped to where his hand rested against the dirty stone floor.

A small puff of dirt blew out of the tunnel. Seeing Luca alive—really alive and not some magical illusion—had made her forget about the collapsing cavern and their too-close proximity. They needed to move. Now. Before the thing buried them in rubble.

"Can you walk? I want to get out of here. We can talk once we're away from this half of the mill. The cavern started to collapse after I banished Marco."

His eyes widened. "Help me up. I can walk."

She stood, reached out a hand, and yanked him to his feet. His fingers tightened around hers as they darted up the stairs and into the last rays of the setting sun.

Chapter Thirteen

An odd combination of shock and relief flowed through Luca as he paused at the top of the stairway. He lived. Really lived. Not some half life of ghost-like transparency. No, his heart pounded a thumping beat behind his ribs, while his lungs breathed in air to survive, not out of habit or part of an illusion, but to keep his heart pumping with life. The evening scent of grass was like manna to his soul.

Humidity clung to his skin, thick and with a scent all its own.

How was any of this possible? Had he died and was now in Heaven? A press of warmth against his palm drew his attention to his hand entwined around Adrianna's fingers. Or maybe she'd freed him.

Which was more likely. What were the odds Heaven resembled the mill?

He gave her hand a squeeze to ensure himself he could. She squeezed back, pausing as her gaze searched his face. If he could touch her, what else could he touch?

Dropping her hand, he reached for the stone column of the archway. Sun-warmed stone rested against his fingertips. He knelt and plucked a piece of grass. Rolling it between his thumb and forefinger, he stared at the green blade as he stood.

For the first time in over a century, he touched

grass. And stone. And human skin. All without being part of illusionary magic.

He grabbed Adrianna's hand and stared at his skin touching hers. Touching hers outside of the cavern, outside of the deception of magic. Freedom came with perks he'd never imagined.

He grinned.

She tugged on his hand, stepping away from the stairs. "Come on. Away from here." Tension laced her voice, a sense of urgency, a tremble of fear.

Whatever worried her couldn't be more shocking than his rebirth. "I can touch you."

"I know. Come on." She glanced behind him. "I want to be out in the middle of the lawn in case the wing collapses."

All right. So he was wrong about her worries being more shocking than him touching her. Being this close to a collapsing building might switch his present state of alive to dead.

And the thought of spending another eternity as a ghost, and a permanent one at that, sent a shockwave of movement through his body.

He wasn't sure which one of them walked faster as they put distance between the mill and themselves. Having just found freedom from spirit form into life, the risk of dying spurred him forward, until she tugged him to a stop.

They stood in the middle of the lawn where they had a clear view of both wings of the mill. Now that he was no longer in imminent danger of dying, the building failed to capture his attention. God only knew he'd spent enough time staring at the damn thing. Instead of watching the roof collapse or a stone wall tumble to the ground, he took in the sunset, the play of light against the greenery of nature. Sensory overload caused him to notice small things he'd taken for granted when he lived before, like the crunch of grass beneath his shoes, the brush of air against his flesh.

The feel of warm female skin against his palm.

Adrianna.

Her silence expanded into the evening, her focus snagged on the mill like cloth on a nail. She held his hand but offered no words besides the request to flee from where they'd previously stood. Why wasn't she amazed at his sudden freedom?

And then an unpleasant set of memories rushed through his mind. Before Marco stole her from his side, her anger had been directed at him. The fact she'd drawn the wrong impression and believed he used her punched like a fist into his chest. He hadn't used her, would never use her, but he had feared telling her about her role in freeing him from the curse. For the very reason she incorrectly believed.

He should have told her long before she reached the conclusion he'd slept with her only to save himself.

Hindsight was everything.

Was she still angry? Was that why she was so quiet?

"Are you still mad at me?" he asked.

Her gaze focused from the mill to him, a fine line running between her brown eyes until understanding flared. Curls bounced against her shoulders as she shook her head. "Not anymore. You should have told me straight up, though. I still would have helped you. But I also realize why you kept it to yourself."

Relief whooshed through him. "I am glad. This is

overwhelming. Being alive. No longer cursed. And no Marco." In a strange way, Marco had helped him adjust to being cursed. Not that he'd ever fully adjusted. But it had helped to have someone there who knew what he was going through. Who listened to him yell, complain, and mourn.

Now Marco no longer existed. At least not on this plane.

"Are you mad at me? For banishing him to Hell?" A stillness fell over her, as if she feared his response.

Hadn't he already told her he was all right with it?

"No. I told you to do it."

"I know. But I also know how much you cared for him."

"I cared for my brother. The creature you banished was no longer my brother. He hadn't been for a long time. It was like a demon from Hell stole him before we were even cursed. The more time passed, the worse he became until evil consumed him." He shook his head. "The thought of him rotting in Hell for an eternity scared me at first until I realized my brother, my beloved older brother, was no longer inside the creature you banished. So, yes, you had to banish him. Or his evil would have only grown."

She gave a sigh of relief. "I'm glad you finally reached that conclusion. The creature I banished was pure evil."

"He wanted you dead."

"Because I'm one of Dario's descendants?"

He nodded. "Yes."

"Ah. Revenge." Her brow furrowed. "Is that why he got so mad when he saw my ring?" Adrianna held up her hand, flashing the red stone in the evening light.

"That's the same ring Dario wore when he cursed us."

One fine brow rose. "Huh. It did do a number on Marco, both at the pool when he attacked me and when I banished him. It doesn't feel magical. Well, okay, it did when I spoke the banishing spell, but not normally."

He shrugged. He might have spent the last century for all intents and purposes as a ghost, but magic and objects channeling magic were out of his realm of knowledge.

Her fingers stroked across the back of his wrist as she gazed at their joined hands. "How can you be touching me?"

"You know how. You broke my curse."

"I didn't do anything but drag you out of the cavern. Even though I thought you'd turn transparent halfway through the tunnel like normal, I couldn't leave you to be smashed if the ceiling collapsed."

He kissed the smooth skin of her forehead, tasting the clay and dirt. "And for that I am grateful. I would not want to wake free from the curse only to be buried in a pile of rocks. And then die."

"Exactly." Her thumb brushed back and forth across his cheek. "I didn't want that either. Thank you for saving me. If you hadn't jumped between Marco and me—"

A shudder shook him at the memory of Marco's face pulled into a gleeful snarl as he readied a killing blast. His grip tightened on her palm. "The sacrifice was worth saving you."

Her eyes widened. "That's it! By saving me you saved yourself. That's how you broke the curse. *That* was your selfless act."

He blinked. And again for good measure. While he knew he had to perform a selfless act on one of Dario's descendants in order to free himself from the curse, he hadn't thought about himself at all in the moment. All he'd seen was a death blast heading toward her, and he'd done the only thing he could think of to stop it from reaching its target—jump between it and the woman he loved.

"You're right." Oh blessed day!

"Of course I am." She grinned, nudging him with her elbow in jest. Then her gaze grew serious. "You mean the blast of energy really killed you? You weren't in some sort of cursed spirit state? Knocked unconscious and no longer able to concentrate on appearing to live with breathing and a pulse?"

He shook his head. "I was dead. Not unconscious. Dead. And you saved me."

"You keep saying that, and it'll go to my head."

His laugh boomed across the lawn, reverberating off the stone walls of the mill, the sound more evidence of his freedom. Freedom. A state he had searched for over the last century and never found. Until today. A thrill of anticipation shot through him, followed by a slap of realization, cutting short his joy.

What was he going to do in the twenty-first century? How would he learn all the technology? Where would he live?

The mill wavered in his vision. *Hold it together, Luca.* He was not going to appear weak and pass out in front of the woman he loved, was he? He drew in a deep breath and followed it up with another one and one more for good measure until the structure stopped shimmering in the dying rays of light.

"You can always stay with me."

Her soft voice snapped his attention off his problems and onto her. Brown eyes sought and held his gaze, a silent way of saying she was there for him. How did she know his thoughts? Did being a medium give her mind-reading capabilities?

He cocked his head to the side. "How did you know what I was thinking?"

She rolled her eyes. "It's written all over your face. Like reading a book." She swung his hand, using their joined fingers to point at the mill. "It doesn't look any different. What do you think? You know its appearance better than me."

The mill? What did the mill have to do with his life in this century? Oh, right. The ceilings had rained dust upon them as she pulled him to safety. They stood in the middle of the lawn to escape a potential building collapse. Amazing how experiencing freedom made him forget the obvious.

Before she thought he experienced a sudden loss of hearing, he swept his gaze over the stone building from the renovated wing to the ruined half. Nothing looked different, but the dimming light made it hard to tell.

"It looks fine to me, but if you are worried, we can go someplace else."

"No, I just wanted to make sure the ruined wing wasn't going to collapse. My apartment has been renovated and is stable. But the cavern and the hall by your room were raining dust and small stones. You can't tell now, though." Her brows furrowed. "I thought for sure a big cloud of dirt would explode out of the tunnel as the ceiling collapsed."

"Maybe it didn't collapse."

"Obviously." She brushed a clot of dirt from her hair.

He looked at her, really looked at her, taking off his rose-colored glasses of freedom to take in her appearance.

Dirt lined her face, caked in her hair, dusted her clothes. A quick glance down his front showed he looked the same, his white shirt a light brown. Perhaps a bath was needed. Despite knowing his freedom allowed him to leave the property, actually doing so frightened him a little. Only a little. A feeling he refused to express. A feeling he would resolve tomorrow.

For tonight, he needed a bath, needed to feel the warm water against his skin, to assure himself he was truly once again physical and no longer a ghost. A long relaxing bath. One to wash the grime from his body and his soul.

"I need a bath."

"A shower." Her brows waggled as she grinned. "We can take one together."

Now there was a thought. "I'd love to."

****

Adrianna woke in a tangle of limbs, arms and legs entwined with Luca. After a hot shower, a late dinner of Maria's leftovers, several hours of explaining the twenty-first century's technological advances complete with demonstrations, they'd crashed. Only to awaken to a rush of exploring fingers and questing lips. Finding love on the other side of the world from New York was not what she'd planned when coming to Italy. But she wasn't about to complain. Falling in love with Luca ranked up at the top of her best-things-ever list.

Had she actually used the word love? Yep, she had. The thought no longer bothered her. Probably because he was no longer a ghost, the sticking point in her debate. Did he feel as strongly for her as she did for him? Would he want to spend his life with her? He'd thrown himself in front of Marco's death blast to save her. His selfless action had to mean something, right?

She knew he liked her. Hell, he'd proven it several times throughout the night and morning, but did that like translate into love?

Luca blinked sleepy eyes, his gaze focusing on hers as a smile played across his lips. "Good morning."

"Hello, there. Sleep well?"

"I slept. For the first time in a century."

"Cursed spirits are like ghosts in that regard, eh?"

"Unfortunately." He licked his lips. "Do you think we could find the cemetery where my family is buried? I'm assuming I can leave since I'm free of the curse."

Leave her? Or leave here? Getting off her ancestral property she totally understood. He hadn't been able to leave since 1910, and the world had changed. Significantly.

"We can try. I can drive."

His brow furrowed. "Is that your automobile sitting in the yard?"

"My car. Yes." She poked him in the chest. "Are you afraid to ride in it?"

He stared at her for a beat. "Of course not. I have never ridden in one, but I read in the papers about the Fiat and when the Model T came out. The…car…was too expensive for anyone in my village to own, but we all enjoyed reading about the inventions. I am looking forward to riding in yours. The design has come a long way in the last century. It now has a top."

She laughed. "That it does." Her laughter died as she thought about where he wanted to go. "Where is your family buried?"

"The papers said the village cemetery. It's not far from here."

"Did they ever come to one of Marco's parties?"

He shook his head. "Never. Not all spirits linger. Most move to a different plane. But you already know that, don't you?"

"You're right." Her grandfather came to mind. He'd told her good-bye shortly after dying, and she had only seen him once since.

The people who thought mediums could contact any dead person at any time as if there were a ghost-generating phone line clearly did not understand how psychics worked.

"Do you enjoy being a medium?"

Did she? "I used to love it." She paused and drew in a deep breath. "Then, after Angela died, I hated it and never wanted to see another ghost." His raised brow had her rushing her words. "Then I met you. And everything going on here fascinated me. You. The parties. Even Marco and his evil self. And I got to thinking, how many other people have evil spirits haunting their homes? I can help those people."

"You learned you no longer hated ghosts."

She nodded. "Yeah. What I hated was making a mistake that led to a client's death. It wasn't the ghosts' fault. It was mine. It just seemed easier to avoid them in order to never go through that experience again. But I really enjoy helping people relax, knowing their loved one is happy in death."

"Or not happy."

"Well, yeah. But that's not too often. Only if their loved one had evil in their soul."

"Like Marco."

"Exactly." Her gaze slid from his, focusing on the pillow behind his head. "Is it wrong for me to say I enjoy knowing I banished him? Not during the actual act. That was pretty damn scary. But later. Is that wrong of me?"

He shook his head. "No. It's your job, and you are good at it. Of course, you will like it."

"So my continuing to be a medium won't bother you?"

"Should it?"

"Well, I'd hope not." A nervous chuckle escaped. "It bothers some people. And if we stay together..." Her voice trailed into silence.

He leaned forward, his lips inches from hers. "If?"

Bam, bam, bam! "Adrianna! I brought dinner. Open up!"

She jumped, bumping noses with Luca. *Ouch!* Painful but not nearly as bad as Maria walking in on them. Damn, the woman's timing really sucked.

He rubbed his nose, his expression the same she knew sat on her face— a bunch of oh-shit.

"Quick!" she whispered. "Get dressed and sit in the chair."

"Adrianna!" Maria banged on the door.

Shit! "Just a minute!"

She rolled the opposite direction from Luca, grabbed her clothes off the floor, and pulled them on as fast as possible. A glance toward Luca showed him hopping on one leg, trying to shove his foot in his shoe.

She ran a hand through her mess of curls.

Good enough. If Maria didn't want to see what was clearly in front of her, then she shouldn't have come over without warning.

Although in all fairness to the older woman, it was the same time she always dropped by.

She flipped the bedspread over the sheets and hurried to the door.

Yanking it open, she grinned at Maria. "Sorry." She stepped back as Maria walked inside.

And froze in the doorway to stare at Luca.

He ran a hand through his hair and offered her a sheepish grin. "Hello, *Signora* Toscano. How are you today?"

Maria's mouth gaped, her eyes popped wide, as she stared at Luca. Then all the color drained from her face as her hands shook. Adrianna grabbed the food container before she dropped it.

"Maria?" She set the container on the floor and touched Maria's arm. "Are you okay?"

One hand pointed at Luca. "I see him! It can't be! He's cursed."

"Was cursed. Wait. How did you know about the curse?"

"Was cursed?" Maria turned to her, small spots of color spreading across her cheeks. "Where is the other one?"

Luca stood, took a step toward them, then stopped at Adrianna's head shake. "You knew about us?"

"How did you know about them? If you knew they were here, why bother to fix the place up and invite me over?" Seriously. Marco could have hurt or killed an unsuspecting non-psychic.

Or even a full-fledged practicing psychic.

Ignoring her questions, Maria headed toward the table and with a heavy sigh plopped onto a chair.

Okay, then. Clearly the older woman was not going to pass out. Or answer her questions.

She shut the door, grabbed the container off the floor, and carried it to the table. After placing it in front of her, she sat across from Maria.

"Maria. Answer me. What is going on?"

Maria glanced to Luca, her eyes narrowing. Luca wisely sat back down on the chair, put his hands on his knees, and gave her his best smile. Maria *humphed*.

"Your grandfather brought you here every summer, and yet you said he never mentioned the mill. I can't believe he didn't tell you about the stories surrounding this place."

"Okay. So Grandfather should've mentioned it. He didn't. That still doesn't explain why you sent me here knowing there was an evil spirit."

"You are a famous New York medium. We thought you'd banish him." She glared at Luca. "I hope this is Luca and not Marco."

Adrianna walked to Luca and grabbed his hand. "Maria, meet Luca Fausto."

Luca smiled. "Hello, *Signora* Toscano. It's nice to see you with living eyes."

"It's been said Dario regretted cursing you." Maria's narrow glare eased. Then grew wide as she glanced from their joined hands to the bed.

Great. She was a grown-ass woman for God's sake. No reason to be ashamed someone noticed she'd slept with a man. So why did she feel like a teenager caught in the act by her parents?

She cleared her throat, which did its duty of snapping Maria's attention from the bed back to her. "Dario gave Luca a way out of the curse, so I suppose he did feel bad about it."

"He should have noticed I was standing there before cursing us." A tic throbbed in the muscle of Luca's jaw.

A little tension clearly remained. Not that she blamed him. If she had been cursed to a ghost-like state for over a century, she'd be a little pissed too. Even if she found the love of her life because of the curse.

A good ending didn't change the fact of crappy circumstances.

Maria *tsked*. "You wouldn't be with her"—she waved a hand at Adrianna—"if he hadn't cursed you. It turned out for the best. You haven't told me where your brother is."

Luca dropped his gaze. Adrianna gave his hand a little squeeze.

"I banished him. Marco's no longer here. In the process it seemed like that wing"—she gestured toward the other half of the mill—"was about to collapse. There were rocks and stones and dirt falling on me as I was trying to escape with Luca—"

"*Dio Mio!* Are you okay?" If Maria's eyes grew any larger, they could double as small moons.

"Yes, yes. I'm fine. Luca's fine. But I'm not sure about the mill. I don't know what else you have planned for renovations, but you might want a structural engineer to check out the place first."

"Oh good. I'm glad you are both all right. Banished him, you said?" At Adrianna's nod, Maria continued. "I'm sure all the rocks and dirt were God scraping the evil clean. But if it makes you feel better, I'll get someone to check it out."

"That would be good."

And now she needed to tell Maria about their relationship. She was thirty-two for God's sake and could tell the woman who was like her grandmother she had a boyfriend.

Really. She could.

"Um, Maria? I need to tell you—"

Maria waved a hand. "Yes. I can see. You two." She grinned, slapped her hands on the table, and stood. "My Luigi and I hoped you'd save this one. Provided he was still worth saving. Rumors said he was a good man and didn't deserve the curse."

"Do you know what my family was told? About Marco and me going missing?"

"Dario's curse brought ruin to the mill. Blew holes in the walls, collapsed the roof. Heard tell it felt like an earthquake. Blaming the explosion and resulting collapse of the mill on an earthquake is what circulated at the time. Or at least that's the rumor passed down over the years. Your parents were told you died in an earthquake that ruined the mill. While they did not have a body to bury, they placed a marker for you in the village cemetery."

"I have a gravestone?"

"Hey, I always knew you were special." Adrianna poked Luca in the ribs with her elbow. "Not everyone can claim their own gravestone. At least not while still alive."

Luca blinked a couple of times at her attempt at humor before his lips twisted into a curve. "I guess you're right."

"Of course, she's right." Maria pointed a finger at him. "And don't you forget it. Well, now, I'm off. Enjoy dinner. I'll see you tomorrow."

She marched to the counter and picked up a couple of the empty food containers Adrianna had cleaned and set aside. Maria gave her a quick peck on the cheek and a long hug before striding out the door to her car.

Okay. Maria's visit had been beyond weird. Luca stood next to her in the doorway, watching as Maria drove off. A fine line etched a path between his brows.

"She knew about Marco and me?"

"Yeah. That was weird. I can't believe she didn't tell me this place was haunted by an evil spirit. She's lucky I stopped him. Not every psychic could. He was pretty powerful."

"Ah, but you are more powerful. And good at doing your job." He glanced from her to the trail of dust indicating Maria's departure. "But I agree. They should not have sent you here without telling you first."

"Well, I'm glad they told me about this place. Even if the telling should've come with a warning." She ran her fingers down his arm, grasping his palm. "I never would have met you if they hadn't invited me to stay here."

A smile curved his lips. "Once again I agree with you." He paused, his gaze searching hers. "I enjoy being with you, Adrianna. I want to stay with you."

"Why?" Her question sounded rude even to her ears, but she had to know. Did he want her like she wanted him? Or did he feel secure around her, safe from the outside world asking too many questions about his past?

Hazel eyes held her gaze. "I love you." As her

mouth fell open, he held up a hand. "I felt this way before you pulled me through the cavern and saved my life. But I did not know how to tell you. I would not have slept with you if I did not care."

A thrill of hope unfurled in her heart. He loved her. Despite her banishing his brother to Hell, he loved her.

Her lips curved into an expression of her heart. "I love you too, Luca. At first, I wasn't sure since you were a ghost. How would that work? Me alive and you, not really? But now that you are alive, we can see where this goes."

"I want it to go for a very long time."

She grinned. "Yeah, me too."

He leaned forward to kiss her, his lips brushing against hers. She wrapped her arms around his neck, but before she could deepen the kiss, he pulled back, brows forming a vee.

"What?"

"Will you continue to help me learn about this century?"

"I'll help you learn all about it. And I'll take you to see your family's burial plots. But first you need to come here." Pulling him closer, she closed the distance between their lips.

Never in her wildest imaginings had she thought she would fall in love with a ghost. Make that a former ghost. Then again, plans changed. And sometimes the things you ran from were the very things you needed.

As the late afternoon sun spotlighted them in a haze of warmth, rays of peace surrounded their hearts, freeing them from the shadows of the curse. Bound in love, they would face any future together.

Love twined through her soul, a love that had

reached across a century to find her. A love she would cherish forever.

A word about the author…

Karilyn Bentley's love of reading stories and preference for sitting in front of a computer at home instead of in a cube drove her to pen her own works, blending fantasy and romance mixed with a touch of funny.

Her paranormal romance novella, *Werewolves in London*, placed in the Got Wolf contest and started her writing career as an author of sexy heroes and lush fantasy worlds.

Karilyn lives in Colorado with her own hunky hero, two crazy dogs, aka The Kraken and Sir Barks-A-Lot, and a handful of colorful saltwater fish. Find out more about Karilyn at:

www.karilynbentley.com